Legend Has It

Sam Silver

Also By the Author

Burning Embers

Meltdown

Incipience

Prologue

Meridian's Line

The cold surface of the carpet presses up against my cheek. Soft, misty tendrils emerge from my mouth, reaching out for the moonbeams that stream in from the window above. The world is blurry, shifting from side to side in a warped haze of nausea.

The cold ripples through me, etching its way into my skin like tiny, tingling claws. I groan. The sound bellows tenfold in my head. The world blurs further. I blink. There are no thoughts. No memories. Something should have surfaced by now, but the more I try to think, the more I hit a flat wall. Everything's swirling and I feel as sick as the bowels of hell.

Instinct takes over and I sit up, only to be greeted by stabbing needles of pain all over my body. To make matters worse, my mind stays blank. I can't retreat into its sanctuary for protection. There are only questions, not answers. Or at least there would be, if the demands of these bleak waking horrors weren't sucking so much out of me. I can't penetrate my mind, my body's in agony, and what lies beyond both of them is far worse.

The night makes it hard to see what's around me, even more so as my vision twists sickeningly at the end of a long narrow tunnel. It's like I'm a speck of dust flitting around in a storm, desperately looking for something stable to latch onto. I turn my head. The world swirls and takes a few moments to solidify. I turn my head the other way. Same thing happens.

The tree branch outside scrapes against the windowpane. The noise stabs into my brain like a steel blade. The rain doesn't help either. Every drop that lands may as well be a gunshot. Even the shadows on the walls look like dancing, mocking hobgoblins.

I put a hand to my temple and wince. My heartbeats are like pounding drums. The breaths I take may as well be gusts of wind sweeping through a chasm, with the opening of my mouth as the entrance to its vast expanse.

My hand presses into the floor.

Squelch!

I raise it, peering at my fingers.

Blood. Stinking, red, thick, sticky, blood.

My stomach heaves. I scramble backwards, hitting the wall behind me with a nauseating thump. Reality kicks in. My tunnel vision vanishes, the world sharpens, and my eyes adjust as the haziness clears, if only a little.

Masses of paper are scattered over the floor, many covered in the blood on my hand. My face too. I feel it on my cheeks.

I look around. Things aren't swirling as much now. That's easing off. My hearing softens, thank god, but it's still impossible to remember anything. I glance at the bloody papers. They're all in piles. Some handwritten, some typed. I shift a bit. It's not easy. My body's heavy and my legs are limp. I try moving one of them.

Squeak!

It hits a chair wheel, then …

Thud!

A heavy shape plummets from the seat, hitting the floor with a sickening squelch.

A body.

With the large handle of a hunting knife smacked deep in its rib cage.

I recoil, scrambling over the floor, sliding over the blood, papers and chaos, making for the nearby door. Finally, I reach the doorknob, pulling hard.

Locked.

I should be terrified, but no. Just the opposite. I'm furious. Ready to kill. This is a setup. Whoever's done this to me'll end up like the body. Splattered to hell. I swear it. Nobody does this to me. All I want, what I truly want, is to grab the knife from the body and turn the killer's face into a screaming, ugly–

2

I stop dead, horrified. Is this who I am? *What* I am? Did I do this? All of this? Is everything here tonight because of me? The only thing that feels real is my growing tsunami of anger that's welling up into a volcanic rage, igniting into—

No! I can't rely on this hate. There's got to be other options. Alternatives. Always.

Somewhere, deep down, through all the blood, chaos and terror, something much lighter tingles in me. It's faint, shallow, and very real. I know it won't be for long. Like everything else around here, it'll soon be swamped by darkness.

I pull on the door again, and then again.

No luck. No sign of any key either.

I hit the light switch. No response. I try again. It's as dead as the body on the ground.

I know this is someone's game. This isn't me. None of it is. It can't be.

Or can it?

What am I? Who am I? Where am I? What the hell's going on? I desperately search my mind for answers. There's still nothing.

I blink and compose myself. There's only one thing to do. I might be a killer, I might be a victim, I don't know, but this can't go on. Someone, either good or bad, will come for me soon. In the meantime, there's only one thing to do. Get answers.

I look around. The sight sickens me. I slowly control my breathing and things settle, if only slightly.

I'm in an office. The office of a writer, it seems. Lying on the floor appear to be rough drafts of their work. Some papers are very basic. Handwritten notes, possibly to be typed up. Other papers, which have been printed out, are filled with scribbles, clearly for further corrections.

A large painting's propped up against the wall at the back of the room. One of a middle-aged woman in the nineteenth century. She sits on a rock with a long pale leg protruding from her skirt. The picture sits, surrounded by papers littered with scattered blood specks.

I look up. A large mahogany desk's nearby. A desk lamp's on it, along with a metal fan with blades to match. What stands out most, is a heavy granite plaque between them. I can just make out in the moonbeams. *Sam Silver.*

I frown. There's an inkling in my brain. An undercurrent. The name's familiar. I reach for the memory. Nothing surfaces. It makes me angry, like a starving beast who's had its dinner snatched away. My irritation grows, welling with ever-increasing fury. I need answers, I need them now, and if I don't get them, someone'll pay. Someone'll–

I suddenly stop. Amidst all the hate, rage, fear and panic, I see a third option. It's faint, yet clear. Another way out. A way of reason and logic. Of getting answers, rather than reacting. I have no idea where this rationale's coming from, but I better use it fast because I sense it won't be here for long.

I am a writer. I know that much. I must be the one who wrote everything lying around here, but am I responsible for the way that corpse ended up? There has to be more to this, there has to. This is a game. A sick game. Maybe if–

Click!

Static erupts loudly through the room. It's coming from a PA system above. It's soft at first, then sharpens. It's piercing. Etching into my brain and assaulting my senses, like millions of squirming insects crawling their way into my earlobes to eat out my head from the inside. The static grows louder, intensifying. The light switch doesn't work, yet the PA system does. Now I understand. This is a set-up.

The static becomes deafening. I want to scream, to yell, to rip out the speaker, wherever it is. I curl up on the floor, blocking my ears to shut out the inferno of noise. My eyes close tightly as I struggle to think of something, anything, to get me out of here.

A defiant spark rises.

"Come on," I whisper, clenching my teeth. "Gimme what you got. Gimme everything!"

The static ripples through my body.

"Is that it?" I scowl. "It's nothing! Are you that scared to show yourself?"

The static stops abruptly. The silence is deafening and my ears ring sharply.

"Bite me!"

The voice is digitised, distorted, and it's impossible to tell if it's male or female. The fact that I've just had an overture of hell's greatest hits drilling into my head doesn't help, nor does my blurred vision.

The voice continues. *"I know you can. You're more than capable of it."*

Capable of what, I wonder.

I look at the body. It almost seems alive in a macabre way. Like it's talking to me through an ugly spirit. No, that's not right. Whoever's behind this is playing games.

The voice speaks coolly. *"We're only at the beginning of your story."*

I observe the papers on the floor.

"It's easy to rip into someone from behind a screen!" I snap, gazing back at the roof. "Why don't you come out here and talk face to face?"

"Maybe I'm afraid of what you'll do to me. It's in your blood."

I swallow hard, feeling the stickiness on my hands.

"This isn't right," I say grimly.

"Yet parts of it feel perfect. Don't they?"

That much is true.

The voice stays as cool as ever. *"Why not admit that you carry piercing inner shards that scare you to death? We all have them. Thing is, if you cage up a wild beast for too long and neglect it, it gets hungry."*

I shift uneasily. No, I reason. Whoever this is, they're not going to pull my strings. No way. I grip the edge of the desk and hoist myself up. It hurts, big time.

"Who are you?" I press. "Why not tell me? Or are you too much of a wimp?"

To my surprise, the voice relents. *"I'm a Meridian."*

"A Meridian?" I ask, unimpressed.

"Yes."

"What's that supposed to be?"

The voice doesn't answer.

A world map on the wall catches my gaze. The smear of a bloodied hand goes down it. The contours waver in my vision. Realisation dawns.

"You're saying you're an imaginary line that makes up boundaries?"

"And boundaries can be shifted," the voice replies, *"depending on where you want to put them."*

"So you're not real?"

"Are you?"

The world blurs in my perception. I look at my hands. They split into four, then eight, then back into two again.

"Is any of this?" I wonder.

The voice likes this.

"Very good," it purrs. *"Now you understand."*

5

I dismiss this. "You're trying to drive me nuts by making me think I killed this guy and that you're a voice in my head."

"I'm saying," the voice says calmly, *"that boundaries are flexible, and people rarely test them. They like to play it safe. You, on the other hand, are capable of so much more."*

I look through the window to the moon outside. Its dim glow's overshadowed by the dark clouds sweeping across it, steadily diminishing its light.

"So where do we draw the line?" I ask.

"Perhaps it's already drawn for you," the voice answers, *"which means you only have to find it. For that, you need to uncover your inner Meridian."*

My gaze turns to the savaged body on the floor.

"And what does the line separate?" I ask softly.

"If you truly embrace what you are," the voice states, *"you won't be thinking of boundaries at all."*

Somewhere in my mind, amidst the dying glow of resistance that's steadily being crushed under the weight of this place, I hear distant laughter. Mocking cackles that are faint, but growing.

"And what am I?" I ask.

"You tell me," the voice replies.

I hate that it's prompting me like this. "All I know is that you're a sick freak!"

"Are you talking to me? Or yourself? Aren't we one and the same?"

The laughter in my head grows louder. The scraping of the tree branch on the windowpane does too. My fingers curl up in anguish.

"Good," the voice whispers, as if reading my thoughts. *"Now you're getting it."*

"Getting what?" I ask, looking around. "I'm not getting anything here!"

"Does that mean you're losing it?"

"Get stuffed!"

The voice doesn't like this. *"Wrong way. Repression's a bad thing. It only makes your inner beast surface with a vengeance."*

I like that I've riled them. "So you've got something to do? Do it! Or am I just listening to a churning toilet bowl here?"

Silence.

"This is garbage!"

"Garbage which you're in the middle of. Look around you."

I focus on the papers that are typed out and lying in separate piles.

"You're in the middle of a much bigger story," the voice says. "One that's being written as we speak."

"By who?" I ask.

"By us."

I indicate the papers. "It looks like *a* story was being written here, but I don't know if it was by me or the dead guy."

"So why not find out?" the voice prompts. "All you have to do is read."

My vision blurs again. The voice's words resonate within me. I have an affinity with writing, that's easy enough to see.

"If you want answers," the voice says, "then read, and keep reading. You'll find out who Sam Silver is, who you are, who the body is, and who I am, but there's a price to pay. Reading isn't always one-way. You see, what we have here is a two-way relationship. One in which things go back and forth. Surprises can pop up. Unexpectedly."

A mocking burst of laughter echoes in my head, care of a vague memory.

"What if I don't want to read on?" I ask.

The response is simple. "Then we both disappear."

"What do you mean by that?"

The voice ignores this. "There are six piles of paper near your left leg. All contain stories. You only have to pick each one up and read them. Aloud. Simple really."

"What for?"

"Because one of them's true."

A jolt of fear goes through me. We're getting to the crux of things at last. "What's the point of that?" I ask. "Why play guessing games?"

"You know where to find your answers," the voice says. "If you want to keep talking, that's fine by me, but it won't get either of us anywhere. No one knows you're here, and you won't be stumbled upon by accident, I'll make sure of that. For things to move forward, you have to read each story. Once you're done, you simply choose the correct one. If you're right, I'll open the door and you can leave."

"And if I'm wrong?"

No response.

I indicate the body on the floor. "Is that what happened to them? Did they pick the wrong one?"

"The answers are written in blood."

I swallow hard. The world swirls again. Maybe the voice is right. Maybe I am insane and in a psychotic episode of an inner horror show I can't wake up from. For all I know, I might have been in a car accident and am struggling to find my way back into my body. I've heard about these things happening.

I quickly dismiss this. It's not what's happening now. I know where my boundaries are, even if this voice, whatever it is, is trying to shift them.

I sigh wearily, dreading to think what'll happen if I walk out the door. There's no choice but to play on. Standing here talking won't do any good. I let my legs go and slump to the floor. My hand moves over to a piece of blood-stained paper.

"So the deal is," I begin, "I pick the right story and you let me go?"

"No," the voice replies, *"you'll let yourself go. In more ways than one."*

I shudder. "So one shot to guess the right story?"

"One shot only," the voice replies. *"Get it wrong and I'll have to step in, literally, and I get mad when things don't go my way, as you can see."*

I don't need to look at the body to know what this nutcase is talking about. "I didn't ask for any of this."

"Nobody asks to be in the story they're in. It just happens. If you want to make it mean anything, you have to follow it through to the end."

"I only want to wake up from this crap."

"You can. A few stories are a touch fantastical, but isn't that life in general? Reality always shifts when a Meridian comes to play."

This is getting too much. "Shut up!"

"Only if you read on. If the story's too way out, you can dismiss it. Choose wisely. You may write off a couple of them straight away, but there's clues in every tale, pointing to the correct one. Don't cut out the heart of the true story, or you'll really know the meaning of a heart attack."

I relent, defeated, and pick up a sheet of paper stained with blood. The moonglow's returned, giving me a little light to read. *The InCreminators*, written by Sam Silver, whoever he is. Could be me, the voice or the dead guy here.

"Tell me a story," the voice prompts. *"Read loudly. I need to know you're not skimming."*

"You just don't want me getting too far ahead of myself."

"A Meridian defines the boundaries."

"I thought there were no boundaries? Story keeps changing, doesn't it? Maybe you're as trapped in here as I am."

A scowl seethes through the speaker.

My spark glows again, like I've just slapped them across the face.

The voice's tone lowers. I can tell it's annoyed, yet it doesn't retaliate. Probably 'cause it knows what's coming, I figure. *"I need to hear your tone as you read. I'd love nothing more than to see you become one with the story."*

The wind grows from outside.

"You wanna talk some more?" the voice asks.

I stare at the paper in my hands. It swirls in my vision. It'll be a headache to read, especially in this dim light, but there's no other option.

"No," I say. "I'd like to see what's coming to me."

"You know what'll happen if you don't," the voice states. *"One way or another, you'll get a bloody great read."*

I peer through the bloodied words on the paper, inhale sharply, and begin.

Chapter One

The InCreminators

"So sad, isn't it?"

"Terrible, my dear, simply terrible."

"Still, it's better she went the way she did, rather than having a stroke. There was no quality of life left. None whatsoever."

"No. None at all."

The two voices trail away as the crowd gathers in the shade of a giant tree. A Moreton Bay fig, surrounded by a low stone wall, which people sit on. It doesn't bring much comfort to anyone from the searing heat of the day. Everyone's sweltering, even in the shade.

My formal attire's stifling. Not only that, everything's blurry. The glare's bright and the voices are intense. My mouth's dry, but it's nowhere near as bad as the roaring headache I've got. The flies are annoying too. I swipe one off my forehead and blink.

The babble of voices continues.

"Have you met my Aunty Gwen?"

"This is Jack. He's a friend from the bush ..."

"It's so nice to meet you ..."

"... I'm in finance now ..."

"Arrgh! The flies are horrible, aren't they?"

"You haven't answered my question."

I pinch the top of my nose, shut my eyes, and do my best to block the voices out.

"I said you haven't answered my question," the last voice repeats.

I open my eyes and look at the elderly lady who sits next to me on the stone wall that surrounds the giant tree. She's looking at me inquisitively from behind her dark glasses.

"Sorry?" I ask, in a parched voice.

"How's your writing coming along?" she asks, repeating her question.

I frown, confused. My headache eases off a little, and everything becomes less intense, apart from the heat, that is.

"Good," I find myself replying. "It's going really well."

I have no memory of her asking the question.

She smiles and nods. "You'll do well, I'm sure. I've always had great faith in you, Sam. In fact I– oh hello!" She turns and talks to another woman on the other side of her.

I look around again. I'm near the admin building of what appears to be a cemetery, with a crowd that's about to form a funeral procession. No one's familiar, and I've no idea of how I came to be here. All I know is that I've just woken up in the middle of this burning day with a massive headache and no memory.

"Oh look," says the old lady, "there's Xavier and Samantha. It's so nice of them to come, especially on such short notice."

She smiles at me.

I smile back, without a clue as to what she's on about, but one thing's clear. This tall, elderly lady in long, white pants and a blue shirt knows me, and is the key to unravelling what the hell's going on. It's an effort to fight against the heat and nausea, but I try and overcome it to make conversation. I swish another fly away and say, "God, I hope it cools down soon."

"Oh yes," she agrees with a nod. "I hate the heat. I don't know what the world's coming to. We had such a long spell of cold weather, the coldest on record, and then suddenly, this! I've never seen anything to like it."

My voice grows stronger. "Yes. Still, it's good of all these people, I mean for everyone, to come."

"Oh yes," she replies, "and it's such a magnificent turnout. She was a lovely lady."

"Hey Sam," another voice says. There's a tap on my shoulder. I look up, seeing a much younger woman in a dark dress.

"How you going?" she asks.

"Good, thanks," I find myself replying.

"I'm so glad you came." She leans down, hugs me warmly, kisses my cheek and rubs my arm. "I know Sally would appreciate it."

Sally? Is this whose funeral I'm at?

"I wouldn't have missed it for the world," I tell her, without a clue what I mean.

"But on such a hot day," she sighs, fanning herself. "It's a scorcher, isn't it?"

The elderly lady leans in and asks me, "Aren't you going to introduce us, Sam?" She glances at the young woman.

"Yeah," I answer. "Sure."

I indicate the older woman to the younger one. "Uh, this is … a very good friend of mine."

"Oh, you're too modest," the elderly woman laughs, and says to the younger one, "I'm Medina."

"Yolanda," comes the reply. "Were you a friend of Sally's?"

"We went back forty years," Medina answers. "I taught her children at Saint Anne's."

"Really? She was so strong in her beliefs, wasn't she?"

"Utterly. Her way was the right way, with no ifs or buts."

"And that's how it should be."

"Absolutely."

They laugh hollowly, with a creepy undercurrent.

"Oh!" Medina remarks. "Who's that?"

"Who?" Yolanda asks.

We all look to the main gate. A man stands in the street, peering in. Their smiles turn to scowls as they glare at him in sheer disdain.

"Just a passerby," Yolanda says darkly.

"Can't have any outsiders here," Medina hisses. "It would ruin everything."

"Would it?" I blurt out.

They look at me, aghast.

I wish I hadn't spoken.

"What did you say?" Medina asks, horrified.

I struggle to find the words. "I-I was …"

12

"There are jokes, and there are jokes," the old lady states firmly. "Clearly you and I don't share the same sense of humour."

I swallow hard and think quickly. "I just wanted to make sure that it was friends and family only."

"Friends and family only," she confirms. "Absolutely."

"Bloody oath," Yolanda concurs. "Literally."

Medina smiles at this remark. I tense up. It's a strange thing to say and sounds creepy.

I look back at the crowd. A pretty woman around my age walks past. She has pale skin, long blonde hair, and a short skirt. Something about her hits me. I know I've seen her before. I try to think where. Nothing surfaces. Only strong feelings.

Yolanda indicates her to the older lady. "Taron's here. Just in time too."

"*Only* just," Medina confirms, as if disapproving of her in general.

A funeral car moves slowly by. A family's inside. A murmur goes through the crowd and everyone starts moving out of the shade and into the searing heat.

"This is it," Medina says, grabbing her handbag.

"Yep," Yolanda agrees. "Showtime."

Both smile happily, like they're eager for it.

A little too eager.

I stand up and step out of the shade. Slight cloud cover's helped ease the heat. Not much, but enough to make things a bit more bearable.

I move with the crowd, heading away from the main building and down a long winding path. Masses of headstones lie on either side. Thanks to those freaky women, I'm cautious about speaking to anyone.

That leaves no option but to go with things.

For now, anyway.

A few sights and sounds seem familiar. I know I've been down this path before. My guts curl with unease. The only comfort I get is from the one girl who stands out in all this madness. Taron.

An elderly gentleman and another young lady walk beside me. The man catches my gaze and says, "Good of you to come, lad." He pats my shoulder.

"Thanks," I reply. "Sally would have wanted it."

"Oh yes, yes," he agrees with a nod. "She was a damn fine woman, a *damn fine woman*."

"Definitely. So many good memories." I pause hesitantly, then ask, "Do you have any favourites?"

"Funnily enough lad, I only knew her briefly. I'm mainly here to support Zina, my daughter." He rubs the shoulder of the girl next to him.

I nod to her. "Hello."

She nods back.

"Sally must have been special to you," I prompt.

She shrugs. "I didn't know her. I only saw her once before she died. In the hospital."

This is weird. From both her and her father.

"She must have made quite an impression on you," I say.

"She did," she replies. "She couldn't talk much by that stage, but she knew what was coming. It freaked her out, poor thing. She was a lovely lady. Perfect in every way. So full of life right up until the very end. How did you know her?"

My thoughts race. "She was a friend of the family."

The crowd comes to a halt as the funeral car stops before the crematorium.

"Looks like we're here," the old man says.

Several black-suited men approach the car and raise the boot. The coffin is pulled out and they lift it respectfully onto their shoulders before slowly carrying it into the building.

I shift into the shade. It's a relief to get out of the heat. Everyone else struggles to do the same. We're all in a hurry to get inside, and there's even slight pushing. Finally, we shuffle into the crematorium, embracing the cool and much-welcomed currents of the air conditioner wafting over us. A few people sigh with relief and wipe the sweat from their foreheads with tissues and handkerchiefs, grateful to be inside.

Something drops into my jacket pocket. I look down to see a pale hand slip away from it and vanish into the crowd. It's impossible to see who it belonged to, especially with so many people around. I feel the outside of my pocket. A paper crunch follows. A note, no doubt. I won't look for the moment. If it's that much of a secret, then I'll have to play things carefully.

The whole sweaty bunch of us are soon inside the building. I let everyone pass as the gentle lulls of Pachelbel's Canon play softly.

The crematorium's filled with several rows of leather cushioned seats. Up the front is a platform on which the coffin is placed. A press of a button will make it descend into the flames below.

There's a couple of doorways in here. An exit sign's over one. A nibbles and drinks area's beyond it, clearly for the crowd once the service is over. My view of its cut off as the door closes.

I move to take a seat.

A sickening dizzy spell hits me and the world swirls as I put a hand to my head, while placing the other onto a seat's black leather cushion for support.

The coffin looks familiar. I can't recall why, but I've seen it before, and know I'm meant to be somewhere else *doing* something else. I glance at the coffin, then jump as a raging darkness suddenly ignites my very soul. Hate. Unrelenting hate. Savage, furious and ready to blow.

The girl, Taron, walks by.

A sharp pain flashes in my head. I clutch my temples and steady myself.

A memory returns.

I'm running. Running through the graveyard with someone. There's screaming. Cries and yells, along with the savage barks of fierce dogs. We're being chased. Chased by–

"If you'd like to take your seats, please?"

The voice comes from a middle-aged woman with short brown hair, standing on a small platform behind a microphone. She's dressed formally, with the funeral service's insignia on her lapel.

The crowd starts to sit.

I shake my head sickly, regaining my senses. I blink hard and move to the back of the crowd and, when no one's looking, I face the side wall, pull the note out, and open it up.

Back row, far left.

I crumple the note up and look there. The girl, Taron, is seated, looking back at me wide-eyed. What's more, she's shaking.

I head over and sit next to her. Luckily, the service isn't packed, and there's a few empty spots here and there. Strangely, I sense that a couple of people are missing but have no idea how I know this.

The announcer speaks again. "Ladies and gentlemen, we're having a few technical problems. If you'll bear with us, we'll be ready in a moment."

The crowd murmurs. I look at the girl. She swallows hard and wraps her hand over mine.

"Do you …?" she begins.

"Do I what?" I ask. "Remember?"

She clutches my hand tightly.

"So," I begin, "what's the deal here?"

"Not now," she says. "It's too risky."

"Fine," I reply. "Let's talk outside."

She inhales sharply. "They won't let us leave."

The old man, who I'd spoken to earlier, sits nearby. He turns around, somewhat crossly, giving a stern glance.

I put my arms on Taron's shoulders.

"Sorry," I tell him. "It's a difficult time."

He turns back.

"Nice going!" Taron hisses to me. She indicates him with a nod. "I doubt he heard us, but this is a formal occasion, remember?"

"I can't remember a damn thing," I whisper. "I was hoping the service might help out."

"Well if you want to know about who's in the coffin, go ahead. They delved into her records and found everything. Now they're spouting it back."

"What for?"

She sighs wearily. "What do you think?"

"I don't know. They like funerals?"

She nods. "Got it in one. Now there's a fluke."

I stare at her in disbelief. "You're nuts!"

"I'm not the one who's woken up with no memory," she retorts. "Both our minds were s'posed to be wiped, or else we wouldn't be paired up like this. Guess they thought we'd make a good couple, decoration wise. They'll leave us alone, unless you screw things up, then your sacrifice'll have been for nothing."

"Sacrifice?" I ask, bracing myself for the worst.

She scans the room, checking that no one's looking. "Mental cleansing, from the pills they rammed down your throat. While you were busy roaring your head off, I hid mine in the side of my mouth. I spat 'em out when I got a chance and played dumb. My brain's fine. Yours is shot to hell."

I frown, confused, then ask softly, "So they wiped my memory and dumped me back in here? Why?"

Her voice lowers. "To make up the numbers until it's our turn."

"Until what's our turn?"

She gives a quick glance, indicating the coffin.

A stab of terror hits me like an ice-pick. "You're kidding me!"

Her tone hardens. "Behave and you'll live longer. Not by much, but it's something. Thank god I got to the mike up there before the service. Screwed it up a bit, giving us a moment to talk before everything goes down, and not just the coffin." She looks ahead again, to get the focus off us. I do the same, then she leans in and whispers, "Okay, this is how we play it. We revert to your initial plan–"

"*My* plan?"

"Your mind's really hit the dustbowl, huh?" She purses her lips angrily. "Those bastards! We just need to work on a few minor details–"

I've had enough.

"I don't get it," I cut in irritably. "I don't get this place, I don't get these psychos, and I don't get why anyone would wipe my mind just so I could watch a funeral before they kill me." I take a sharp breath. "You know who I do trust? Me."

"You're starting to sound like your old self."

I tense up.

The woman behind the microphone speaks. "Ladies and gentlemen, my name's Morganna Kentworthy, and today I'll be taking you on a remarkable journey through the life of Sally Orelia …"

"I'm outta here," I whisper to Taron.

I stand up and head for the door.

Several people watch me go. Murmurs ripple through the crowd and I get a few death glares. I don't care. I'm gone.

No one rises to bring me back to my seat. The woman up front doesn't say anything. Nobody calls out to me either, meaning Taron's as crazy as the rest of them. The woman keeps talking. Business as usual.

Swearing under my breath, I walk outside.

I step out of the building's cool air-conditioned comforts. The heat sears over my face once more. I brush a fly away and walk down the long, winding path, pushing myself into the sunlight. It's excruciating, but I don't care.

The building falls further behind me. The heat's horrific, though not as bad as my vision, which blurs again. Maybe Taron's right. Maybe a drug's been shoved into my system, making me forget everything.

Things grow blurrier. I step into the shade of a large tree and rest my hand on a headstone to take a breather. Things settle. Not by much, but every little bit helps.

I rub my eyes and look at the headstone.

Its engraving hits me like a thunderbolt.

In memory of Sam Silver.

I stare in horror at the words. My heart beats rapidly. My breaths grow shallow. Time freezes. That name's familiar. Sam. It's what those ladies' had called me when I'd woken up. That's my name. I'm sure of it, but why would it be on a headstone in the middle of a graveyard? Am I Sam Silver? Or did I take his place?

A searing pain shoots through my temples as a memory flickers.

I look down at the same headstone from up in the tree. I steady myself on its thick branches as the savage barks of vicious dogs grow deafening. Crunches follow as they leap high, snapping at me, before dropping onto piles of dry leaves.

Human cries rise.

Running footsteps approach.

I'm pulled out of the tree and dragged away. The dogs are held back as I'm wrenched through the graveyard towards ... towards–

A hand clamps over my mouth. I yelp as I'm pulled to the ground behind my headstone, struggling hard.

A voice hisses in my ear. "Great way to get us both killed, dipstick!"

Taron.

I slap her hand away irritably.

"He nearly saw you," she scowls.

I peer up over the headstone. A solidly built man's in the distance, scanning the area. What stands out most is the heavy gold chain around his neck, complete with a small skull in its centre.

She pulls me back down crossly. "Do you have a death wish?"

I ignore her and ask, "Who's he? A groundskeeper?"

"Technically, yes," she answers. "He's also the security 'round here. An ex-bikie they call the Guardener. You left the service right on time. He'd usually be outside to take you straight back in, but you were lucky he was pulled away by a phone call. Saw him answer it myself. Bet it was about that undercover cop hanging 'round the main gates right before the funeral kicked off. The Guardener probably went to check it out."

I think back to how the two ladies had been scowling at the stranger. Nevertheless, I'm glad Taron's here.

"So you do care about me," I say with a smirk.

She shrugs. "Never could leave you alone. I stayed at the service for a bit, purely for show, then thought, stuff it." She looks sideways. "Had a quick sneak 'round our old hidey-hole a few hours ago. Our stuff hasn't been touched. We'll make for there."

"Hang on, what hidey-hole? What stuff?"

She peers over the headstone once more. I do the same. The Guardener's turned and is heading away. She creeps out from behind our cover, pulling on my arm. "Move."

I don't want to go but have no choice. We head into the heat. It's horrific, and I sweat profusely.

"Where we going?" I ask.

She looks ahead. "The Crucible. We were making for it when we were caught."

"Nice name. What is it?"

"I call it the headstone of resistance."

"So it's got stuff that'll help us?"

"Totally. Darts for one thing. They'll knock anyone right out. Dogs included."

"Sounds like we were prepared."

"We were, until we were sold out."

"Hope the guys who did it aren't around."

"Not after what you did to them."

I grimace. "Sounds nasty."

"You were, believe me."

I wipe my forehead. "I hope you've got some water at this Crucible, or whatever it's called."

"Yeah," she replies. "Not the toxic stuff they dish out either."

"They put something in the water?" I ask.

"That's how we got here in the first place," she answers. She moves into the shade of another tree and turns to face me. I step into the welcoming coolness of its branches as she continues.

"All this started when we got calls at our jobs telling us that a colleague had died. Apparently, they'd wanted us at the funeral, which was an outright lie. We hadn't seen them in years. We each came alone, went to the service, and then drank the spiked refreshments in the foyer. Luckily, we were so caught up talking to each other, that we didn't drink much. Guess first impressions really do count." Her lips flicker with a smile at the memory. "Good thing too. That crap dulls the mind, making people compliant." She pauses. "We saw what was going on and played along ... for a while. Those freaks found us out and went hardcore. They took us to a god-awful shed to force pills down our throats. They wanted us to forget everything, hence why your brain's kissing a blank wall right now."

I purse my lips, so wanting to smash that wall in. "So who's the genius behind this crap?"

She starts moving away.

I grab her arm and whirl her around. "Answers! Now! Before—"

I stop dead, realising I have a strong urge to savagely rip her to pieces. The heat of the day inflames my rage even more. God, she's killing me! I just want to grab a knife, hold her down by the throat and slash her over and over until ...

She stares deeply into my eyes, unfazed. She peers in further, searching, searching, searching for ...

"You're getting there," she murmurs.

My temper eases. Slightly. "Getting where?"

She frowns. "You're almost your old self. Not sure if that's a good or bad thing." She inhales sharply. "Still, you do the right thing. Not like the freaks 'round here. They lure people to funerals, drug 'em up, make 'em sit through a couple of services to keep up the numbers, then kill 'em. They're obsessed with death."

"So how can this place stay open?" I ask, baffled.

"'Cause all the other funerals here are legit. They only have 'Underground' agents scouting them for new targets. Their job's to get as many victims as they can into the crematoriums. There's a name we made up for them, plus all the nutjobs at the psycho service. We call 'em InCreminators." She draws a sharp breath. "And guess what? We were next on the list."

I shake my head. "So what happened? We tried to run, got caught, and they hit me with the drug?"

She looks behind us. "We've got company."

Savage barks erupt in the distance.

I look back with a start.

Four Dobermans are bounding our way.

"Knew it wouldn't be long," she says worriedly.

We lunge out into the burning day. The dogs are more than double our speed and bound over the stones, flying after us.

"There!" Taron cries, indicating a massive headstone ahead. Larger than the rest, it sits under a Moreton Bay fig, and there's a dome on its peak, looking like it can be removed, but with a great deal of effort.

"The Crucible!" Taron calls. "It's—"

Her foot catches on a giant tree root and she drops hard.

I stop to help her.

"Forget it!" she snaps. "Go!"

I run ahead, leap onto the grave and reach the dome. The thing's huge. Calling it heavy's an understatement. I can see why it's the best hiding place. No dog could sniff anything out here. A good plan but annoying me to hell right now. I twist the top with a heave and it shifts slightly.

"Hurry!" Taron yells, leaping up and scrambling for the giant tree. I know she won't make it.

The barks grow louder, inflaming my rage. My animal instinct rises again, inflamed by the heat and the snapping beasts behind me. All I want is to see them ripped to shreds, splattered all over the graves.

I groan and push the dome harder. The lid scrapes loudly to the side, making a gap I can just get my arm into. I reach into the darkness grimly, feel around, and find a knapsack.

The dogs are almost upon Taron.

I wrench the bag out of the small gap. A dart gun drops out. I grab it in mid-fall.

A dog leaps, diving for her.

She screams.

Thuk!

My aim hits home. God knows how. The dog's leg jerks and it recoils with a whimper. The other dogs halt, allowing Taron to scamper up the tree.

The dogs fire up again, sweeping in for me. I climb on a headstone, stand up, grab onto a thick tree branch and pull myself up next to Taron, bringing the knapsack. We steady ourselves as I take out the other darts and reload the gun. Strangely, I can do it automatically, with military-like precision. I've no idea why my reflexes are so good, only that they're naturally ingrained in my muscle memory.

Snap!

My aim's spot on again, freaking me out further. Another dog's hit in the leg and it recoils.

I reload the gun.

"Good to see you've still got your aim," Taron quips.

Snap!

Another dog falls.

"Don't ask me how," I say back.

I load the final dart. Only one chance to get this right.

Snap!

Bang on target. The dog sluggishly hits a statue and passes out with the other three.

"Good stuff," Taron says. "Beats us having one foot in the grave, doesn't it?"

Another cry erupts from far off. The Guardener's spotted us and is running in. That's not easy with the skull chain 'round his neck.

Taron jumps out of the tree and I follow. We bolt deep into the graveyard and shoot down a slope into a mass of giant headstones. We outrun him easily, and when we've finally gained enough ground, we take shelter behind a shrub, looking around quickly.

I indicate the dart gun.

"Where'd we get that sucker from?" I ask, grateful that the dogs are taken care of.

"Guardener's private stash," she responds. "You pinched and hid 'em. We were almost home free when the bastard found another lot to hit us with. We woke up in his shed right before he shoved those pills into our mouths. You caused so much of a ruckus that I could spit mine out without him seeing, right into his bitch-terrier who nearly choked on it."

"Let me guess, I gave him hell to give you a chance?"

"Yeah. You nearly got free too."

"Seriously?"

"Dead serious. You rammed his head into a vice and told him about the job cuts coming his way."

"I don't want to know," I cut in. "Didn't work, huh?"

"Not once he screwed things up for you. Your fingers still sore?"

"I hadn't noticed."

"Then don't. Your funeral was planned as a special event. They wanted you conscious when the coffin dropped you into the furnace."

I grimace. "What kind of funeral's that?"

"They wanted to call it the ultimate *wake*."

I cringe at the thought, then see her gaze. I know there's more to this story. She's wondering whether to tell me or not. That's obvious.

She scrambles around the headstone. "Time to get back to the land of the living."

"Yeah," I agree, following her. "I've had enough of this sick 'State' of Termi-*Nation*."

She nods and we head on.

We make our way through the graveyard, heading for the main path. We barely reach it when a funeral procession, led by a black car, rounds the bend. Taron pulls me behind a headstone and we duck for cover.

"Not friendlies?" I ask.

"They are," she answers, "but there are scouts among them. I know the faces."

"They'd be good at their job then. Getting fired from it would be the ultimate burner."

The procession passes. When they're gone, we move along the opposite path, heading for the main admin building.

The world blurs in my vision and I stumble.

Taron leans in, helping me along.

"That's the toxin," she says as we walk past an empty grave. "The heat makes it worse. Hang in there. Won't be long before we climb out of the hole we've been dug into."

I nod sickly.

The walk's sweltering.

Relief sweeps over me when I see the front gates. We move quickly and soon round the main wall, into the car park.

I break away from Taron and start to make some distance. Only then do I sense her absence and look back. She's not following. She's standing by the fence, looking in.

I stop in my tracks. "What's up?"

She swallows hard, gazing at the mass of graves inside. "We can't leave."

I throw an arm up in disbelief. "Why the hell not? You want to go back in?"

"Yes."

She's dead serious.

I head over to her, ignoring the heat. It's still hot, horribly, but not as bad as it has been. Despite my thirst, I'm not as dizzy now. Whatever's in my system has sweated itself out and I can think more clearly. Strangely, I'm starting to feel tougher.

Heated.

Enraged.

"What's up with you?" I snap. "We can go to the cops and end this."

"Like hell!" she snaps back. "We can't run. We'll be on a hit list no matter where we go. We'll always be paranoid freaks looking over our shoulders. Besides, these funeral fanatics are dead smart. They've covered their tracks and have contacts everywhere. So many people in so many places. Cops, law-yers, military personnel, all ready to take us ..." She glances at the graves. "Downtown."

"We're not in 'em yet," I counter. "Let's split."

"Forget it," she says resolutely. "I'm burying this place."

"You've got a plan?"

"No, but you had a good one."

My face drops.

She scowls. "You've gone soft. The old Sam would've never let anyone take his spotlight. He was always ready to strike back." Her face hardens. "I have to stay. It's what he would have wanted."

I shudder. "I don't like who I was."

She shrugs. "There's the good and the bad. What's back there, though, is evil." She sighs wearily. "I want to stop running. I want peace, and not the everlasting kind."

I nod. "Yeah, I see your point." I look at the main road. "Guess there's no other way. If I run and you fail–"

"You're a dead man," she finishes. "This plan takes two. We'll need to head to the warehouse over the road for a few items, then we're good to go. The longer we wait …"

"I know." I pause. "You're right. We don't have a choice."

"No," she says firmly. "We don't."

My head rises, not liking where this is going. "So tell me, what did I have in mind?"

We head across the street to the warehouse, suspicious as hell of everyone.

Taron has a visa card she's pulled from the knapsack. We buy what we need and return to the graveyard. Skilfully, we sneak past the security cameras covering the entrance and cautiously make our way through the grounds.

We find the Guardener's shed. No memories come up for me and I'm grateful for that. Even better is there's no sign of him, and we use the tools we've bought to break in.

A chemical lab's inside. The foul fumes smell toxic. Clearly, this is where the drugs used to wipe my memories were created.

Taron grabs the drugs we need while I keep watch for the Guardener. Not just from the window but on the camera feeds he's got on a few screens. They cover a large area, including where the funeral-goers, or InCreminators, are. Another shows the dogs still sleeping and will be for a while. I ask how we weren't spotted running through the graveyard. She tells me she knew the camera positions outside, and once upon a time, I did too.

No one else shows up, but I know they will soon. Her disabling of the shed's security camera's bound to raise digital alerts. I tell her to hurry up. She gives an irritable retort and scouts around the shed. Finally, she finds what she's looking for, then uses the PC to print out a document. She tucks it safely away on herself and we quickly tidy the shed, making it seem untouched.

Our work complete, she grabs a set of keys by the table, we head outside, lock the door, and get the hell out of there.

An hour passes. A long hot hour of staying out of sight until the crematorium's empty. When the coast is clear, we make our move.

We enter from the back, care of the keys from the Guardener's shed. Working fast, we fill several jugs of water and mix in the Guardener's drugs. We leave the jugs on a table near the main doors, along with plastic cups filled to the brim. Finally, Taron places her printout on the speaker's stand. With everything in place, we hurry outside and hide behind a headstone, observing the building's entrance.

Shortly after, Morganna Kentworthy approaches and stands in the doorway, watching a funeral procession make its way down the hot, winding path towards her.

The Guardener emerges from the grounds, heading up to her.

She glances around, frustrated. "No sign of them?"

"None," comes the reply. "They were spotted in the warehouse across the street. Buggers were too quick to keep track of."

My heart nearly stops.

"Told ya," Taron whispers, nudging me.

I jump and nudge her back. "Don't do that."

Morganna frowns. "Whatever could they be doing there?"

The Guardener's face hardens. "The girl must have overridden our drugs and turned the boy. Won't be by much. Those couple'a extra pills'll see to that."

Morganna nods. "His personality's softened, by all accounts, but he's still just as dangerous. No matter. Our Scouts are on stake-out." She peers ahead at the funeral-goers. "Still, we have another service, thanks to you." She looks at him. "No witnesses?"

"None," he replies. "Bullet to the brain took care of him. Moron was pathetic for an undercover cop. Hanging 'round the front gate like that, what an idiot."

"Yes," Morganna agrees coolly. "We'll need to contact his family and friends for the commiserations. Gosh knows we need it. With the way our burial business is making a loss we're on the verge of going under." She inhales sharply. "Still, we have an obligation to our investors, and I always provide a good service. Keep me informed."

"Will do."

He heads out into the grounds, striding away from us.

I lean into Taron, speaking softly. "Don't ever tell me what I was like before my mind-wipe, huh?"

"It'd probably kill ya," she quips.

We creep around the building, enter through the back and make for a circuit board.

The doors open and the crowd shuffles in.

The temperature's cool, at first anyway. Bit by bit, it grows. Nobody notices. Soon, everyone starts dabbing their foreheads, fanning themselves and sweating profusely. They reach for the plastic cups of water on the table, delving into them with great swallows. We hear it all from beneath that table, hidden by a draping cloth. Taron loves the risk. I hate it. Too close for comfort for my liking.

We peer through a gap, seeing Morganna Kentworthy who, like most people, dabs her forehead with a handkerchief. "Ladies and gentlemen, I'm extremely sorry about this. We seem to be having trouble with the heating system. If you'll please give us a moment ..."

An Incriminator hurries out the back and works the switchboard. The heater dies and the hum of the air conditioner rises, filling the building with a welcome rush of cool air. Sighs of relief follow.

"Ah, that's much better, isn't it?" Morganna says, as relieved as everyone else. She pulls a water bottle from her bag and takes a big drink. "I apologise for the delay. We'll begin in just a moment." She puts the water bottle down and composes herself, attempting to look as sincere as possible.

The crowd takes their seats, settling in.

Silence falls, then Morganna speaks, reading from the paper on the podium. "Ladies and gentlemen, your willingness to brave such heat today is a testament to your character in paying tribute to our dearly departed loved one. Today, on this sombre occasion, we celebrate the life of Morganna K–"

She stops dead. Her face drops and she gasps, shocked. She scans the notes. "Who's sick joke is this?"

A groan comes from the back of the room.

An old man slides out of his seat, hitting the ground.

She looks up in horror as the crowd gasps.

Another man slumps to the side, sprawling on his wife's lap. She barely reacts before her eyes roll up and she too passes out.

A young lady hits the ground.

A big man and his wife follow.

Two more people drop like stones, with the two behind them keeling over.

Groans and thumps erupt throughout the crematorium as the funeral lovers slump to the floor, leaving a mass of bodies strewn everywhere, making it look like a war zone. A final thud follows, leaving no one conscious, save for Morganna, Taron, and myself.

Morganna looks around, horrified.

"I don't understand ..." she whispers. She steps shakily off the speaker's platform and onto the floor.

Taron emerges from under the table and rises. She glares at Morganna scornfully. "Now there's a burner. Not scared to death, are you?"

Morganna's jaw quivers.

With no choice, I crawl out from under the table and stand by Taron. She'd never said anything about revealing herself so fast.

Morganna glares at us. "How dare you—"

"Drop dead!" Taron snaps bluntly. She indicates the bodies. "Look at this, huh? The funeral director who's dug herself into the biggest hole of all. No need to worry about your business dying now. You can have all the funerals you want."

Morganna and I look at her in disbelief.

"What?" we ask together.

Taron stares back coldly.

Shaken by her ruthless streak, I go over to a man on the floor, kneel, and place a hand on his neck.

There's no pulse.

I stand and face Taron angrily. "What the hell did you do?"

Her gaze rips through me like an icy dagger. "Took a different lot of drugs and learnt how to lie from the best."

Morganna drops to the floor, her eyes welling with tears. "You killed them. All of them. Why. *Why?*"

Taron shrugs. "Guess we like funerals."

Morganna quivers. "Tell me. Please!"

Taron indicates me. "Wasn't my plan. It was his."

"Get stuffed!" I snap back.

"The old you!" she snarls.

I jump at the fire in her eyes.

Her voice hardens. "You've changed for the worst, Silver. You've lost your guts."

"So have they!" I retort, glancing at the bodies.

She scoffs. "Oh yeah, great plan! Knocking 'em out, chucking a shedload of evidence on 'em and calling in every cop on the force aint gonna solve nothin'!" She steps in. "Sure, they'll look into it, but I told you, I *told* you, there's InCreminators *everywhere*!" She scowls. "Keeping this lot alive meant they'll have got out in no time. That's too big a risk!" She glances at the bodies. "Now their buddies out there'll know that things have gone belly-up. Great message, huh?"

"Making us killers!" I growl. "Every cop out there, dodgy or not, will come looking for us now. We'll be locked away, some freak'll find us and we'll be screwed." I motion to the window and the tombstones beyond. "We're already in a grave state and you want to dig us in deeper?"

She seethes furiously. "I remember, man. I remember you on the floor of the Guardener's shed, squirming as the drugs he'd pumped into you kicked in. I'd spat mine out into his bitch-terrier who guzzled 'em and stumbled outside. He went out there to fix things and you said to me, you *made* me swear, that no matter what happened, or what you became after the crap in you when into full swing, that those who did this *would pay*! You were against any thought of them being saved. This, all of this ..." she motions to the bodies, " ... is your baby. Well done, *daddy*!"

The slimy, bubbling nausea wells in me again, ready to erupt. It sickens me to the bone, making me feel like I'm at death's door and I hate it.

Morganna trembles. She looks over the bodies, distraught, and says softly, "They're so beautiful. So ... peaceful. Death always is." She stares up at us wide-eyed. "The end brings people together. When a person dies, there's only peace. No fighting. Only unity. No hate, just love. We celebrate the deceased."

Taron speaks bitterly. "You're a joke lady. Look around. Everyone's corpsing with laughter."

Morganna's tone softens. "Nobody understands. Nobody. It takes a death-changing crisis for everyone to wake up and unite. Peace comes from tragedy. Sorrow. Nothing more." She hangs her head sadly. "They were all good people."

"They were killers!" Taron snaps. "All of them!"

"No!" Morganna hisses. She rises to her feet and steps in menacingly. "They were noble! They saw a greater vision! You've ended their work."

The main door bursts open and the Guardener runs in. He stops at the sight of the bodies on the floor, then sees us. He pulls out a gun, taking aim.

"Business is booming," he growls.

I gaze back at him, showing no fear. I'm not giving this moron the satisfaction. "Shouldn't you be happy your business is back in the black?"

He stares at me curiously. "You've changed your tune haven't you, son? You were eager to get in on it all."

"Must be something in the water," I reply. "Y'know, that stuff you rammed down my throat? Thanks for that. Helped a lot."

He sneers. "There's psychos', then there's you, Silver. I'm nothin' compared to who you really are. That's off the scale cruelty." He shakes his head. "Shame it had to go, but you'd have only made a power grab. Drugs were the only solution. They were meant to make you our ultimate Scout. Our best investment *ever*."

"Yeah," I retort. "So you could 'coffin up' the goods." I look at Taron. "This better not be a power grab on your part."

She too, shakes her head. "We talked about it, but no. Not anymore. There's other things at stake now."

"Like what?" I ask, tensing up.

She glowers. "I want this to be over, Silver. I've had enough to last me a lifetime."

Morgana's head rises. "You were never proud to be of service, Mister Silver. Neither before or after your conversion. You were reviewed by two Scouts when you awoke by the main gate, leaving us with no other choice but to put you on our death list." She sneers cruelly. "Now, we'll have to cut our losses, and I do mean *cut*." She nods to the Guardener.

He smirks cruelly, ready to shoot.

I glimpse at Taron nearby. Her eyes are wide, terrified as hell. For a girl so tough, who'd let nothing get to her, this is illuminating. Even more so when I realise that I'm feeling the same way. My heart thumps. Weirdly, nothing else matters but … Taron.

No, I vow. I'm not dying for anything.

I'm living. For everything.

His finger tightens on the trigger.

I lunge to the side, pick up an urn and hurl it at him, smacking his gun arm off target.

Bang!

The gun goes off as Taron and I drop to the floor. The bullet hits a window high above, sending shattered glass falling around us.

Taron looks at the vessel I'd thrown at him. "That's one way to urn a living."

I leap up, flying into him. His gun clatters to the floor. Scowling, he picks me up and slams me onto the table.

Nearby, I see Morganna dive on Taron. They struggle furiously, falling sideways, but my vision's cut off as the Guardener hoists me up, smashing me against the wall. The sickening thud rips through my spine as I slide to the floor. He goes with me, his fingers clasping my neck while his free hand reaches for the gun nearby. His grip's strong. My eyes bulge out of their sockets, like blobs of veined mush over an open mouth, gasping desperately for air. The skull chain on his neck swings in, hitting my forehead before recoiling and glaring sickly at me. He finds the gun and brings it up. I push it away with one arm while fighting back with the other, then …

Bang!

The gun goes off again, blasting past his ear. He recoils, jolted by the shock. The air floods back into my lungs as relief sweeps over me. I roll to the side, coughing and gasping as my eyes return to their sockets, albeit painfully.

The Guardener winces as blood trickles from his ear.

Taron, however, looks ahead wide-eyed.

Morganna stands motionless, looking aghast. A blood trail flows down her forehead from the bullet wound in the centre. Somehow, through it all, she manages to speak in a muddled confusion.

"I feel … like death …" Her eyes roll up and she gurgles, "… warmed up."

She falls back over the coffin, hitting a button on the way.

Whirr!

The coffin descends into the furnace, carrying her with it.

The Guardener roars, lunging at me.

I scramble up, leaping aside.

He follows, letting loose with a swing.

I duck, he trips on the edge of the speaker's platform and falls onto Morganna's body and the lowering coffin. His skull chain gets caught in the fall and he struggles wildly as his extra weight unhinges the lowering mechanism and he's pulled down.

The flames rise to greet him.

Taron and I cringe as he's dragged into the searing abyss, screaming hysterically in blood-curdling death cries. A nauseating howl follows as the furnace embraces him completely, frying him alive.

Whoosh!

A fireball billows high, releasing the charred smell of burnt flesh.

We watch as it dissipates. No more flames follow. A piercing, mechanised squeal nearly bursts our eardrums and then …

Silence.

Dead silence.

Waves of smoke, ash, and flesh flakes waft through the crematorium. Sickened, I wave a cloud away.

Taron looks to where the coffin had been and sighs wearily. "Well he sure InCreminated himself."

I grimace, then look to the window and the day outside. I've no idea who I was before waking up near the main gates, but I'm glad I'm not him now. Any residue of his blazing anger simmers away, leaving me with nothing but pity for these bodies on the floor.

"Guess they finally got what they wanted," I say softly. "Death."

A metal crank erupts from the furnace, like something's jammed. I look back as the crank grows louder and …

Whoosh!

Morganna's hideously charred skull, complete with a bullet hole in her forehead, shoots up high, falls, and clanks onto the table before us, grinning macabrely. I shudder and turn away. "Talk about getting fired."

Taron does the same, blinking out the ashen smoke. "Yep. She's done and dusted."

I run a hand through my hair in disbelief. She steps in, swallows hard and our eyes meet. I know what she's thinking. All this is mind-blowing. Words can't express the insanity. I inhale sharply, knowing that all we have now, is each other. "Thank god that's come to an end."

Her tone's sombre. "For them. We have to live with it. Til the day we die."

I shake my head. "Enough about death. Let's talk about life."

She frowns curiously. "You've changed your tune. The old you would have gone power-mad by now …"

I raise my hand, stopping her. "I don't want to know who I was."

She bites her lip. "What if I could tell you who you were going to be?"

"What do you mean?"

She pauses. "There … uh … hasn't been time to fill you in on a lot since you woke up. You only got the condensed story. Quite a bit happened before you changed into …" She raises her hand, indicating me "… This."

I don't like where this is heading. "I–"

"Relax," she cuts in. "There were good times too."

"Good times?" I ask in disbelief. "Seriously?"

She nods. "Yeah. What you haven't realised yet, doofus, is that when we first got called away from our jobs and came to this dump, we didn't just show up, get brainwashed, and then sit drugged-out through a few services. We lived here. On these grounds …" Her voice softens "… For three months."

I blink, surprised. "Are you for real?"

"Hey, they wanted you as their head Scout, but you're a tough nut to crack. The biggest nut of all, they said." She seems impressed. "So yeah, three months. Getting dart guns and hiding 'em in headstones doesn't happen overnight. That aint easy when you're living in this place for weeks on end. We did it though. Along with …" She goes silent.

I tense, ready for the worst.

"What?" I ask, bracing myself.

She pauses. "A tomb is for the dead. A womb, however, is for …" Her voice trails away and she rubs her stomach gently.

Reality hits home as I gaze at her speechless. My lips quiver and I blurt out, "You're sure? I mean, you totally know you're …"

She smiles and rubs her stomach again. Her smile grows as she stares deep into my eyes, like she's making the ultimate vow, and says, "I do."

I blink, startled. "Did I … he … I mean the old me …"

"No," she replies. "He didn't know a thing. I'm glad you do." She takes my hand, placing it on her stomach.

A kick comes from within.

I smile, loving every second. There's hope for both of us now. A chance for a new life and a better tomorrow.

Clunk!

Morganna's head thumps to the floor loudly, enough to wake the dead. I look at the mass of bodies strewn over the crematorium, then see a funeral card on the floor. I look grimly at the insignia and say darkly, "This isn't over. We haven't got everybody. As much as we want this kid, we're not safe wherever we go. There's InCreminators, Scouts and god knows who else …"

"Hey," Taron cuts in, grabbing my chin and returning my face to hers. "We're fighting for life now. Our family's. We're not giving in." She glances at Morganna's skull and the hole in its temple. "She bit the bullet. Not us."

I wince and place a hand on my forehead.

She peers in at me. "You okay?"

"Just a headache," I answer.

She nods. "Oh yeah, the memory drugs. They've got side effects, 'specially with you." She brushes my cheek. "You had more than a double dose. Your memory might go again, but only for a little while, I'm sure of it. You'll be fine."

I shake the nausea away. "I know." I gently rub my hand over her stomach. "We all will."

She takes my hand and smiles.

I smile back as we turn and make for the exit. "Let's get out of here. This place is as dead as."

The house creaks under a fierce gust of wind, bringing me back to reality, or whatever the hell this is. I was so caught up in the story that I'd forgotten about this cesspool. Now I'm not even sure if this dump's real, leaving me to wonder if the Merdian's sick voice really exists, or is just my own psychosis.

I look down at the bloodied papers of what I've just read and think about it. Logically, it fits with *everything* here. Completely. The drugging, the memory loss, it's totally InCreminating work. The body on the floor not so much. That's a spanner in the works, screwing this whole thing up. Maybe I'm not Sam Silver but a psychotic InCreminator. There's also enough to indicate that the funeral service is far from dead, but it's hard to tell.

The speaker crackles. No voice comes through. I know it's pressing me to move on to the next tale. That's easy to see. I grimace, wondering if I should call its bluff by saying this story's real and have the whole damn thing over. Please, part of me pleads with myself. Just say it and end this now. Do it. There's too much pain otherwise.

No, my rational side reasons. There's too many questions and five stories to go. Worse still is that they could make *more* sense.

I think back to what Meridian's said.

"There's clues in every tale."

I pick up the next story and look at the title.

InHuman Growth.

Meridian's voice returns.

"A few stories are a touch fantastical."

Going by the title, this one seems that way, but I've got no choice. If it's true, great. If it's not, it's clues might help a bit.

Unless I'm wrong.

Dead wrong.

Grimly, I start to read.

Chapter Two

InHuman Growth

"Hi."

"Hey."

"Guess this is my seat."

"Guess so."

I sit down next to the young woman. She's a looker, to say the least. Her long, auburn hair flows over her bare shoulders onto her red dress. I smile as the wedding guests move past us, towards their tables.

"Looks like I've been placed with you," I say.

"You single too?" she asks.

"Uh ... yeah," I reply.

"I'm gonna kill someone." She smirks cheekily and looks across the ballroom, raising her eyebrows. No doubt at a friend for putting us together, I figure.

"Nice to meet you," I say. "I'm uh ..."

My mind goes blank. I've forgotten my name. I look at the place card before me and read from it.

"Sam," I tell her. "Sam Silver."

She smirks again. "I'm Karmady. With a K."

I nod. "This'll make a fun night. There's nothing like a good Karmady, after all."

"Oh yeah, like I haven't heard *that* before," she replies. "And I'm not that good, but am good at what I do." She picks up an open wine bottle. "Which is party. I'll get straight into this." She pours the rich, red drink into her glass and sips it. "Hmmm. Not bad."

I see the name on her place card. *Karmady Wheeler.* Odd name, I think, but she's fun enough to fit it.

Another chair's pulled out and a guy, my age, sits at my other side. He tenses, speaking nervously. "Hi."

"Hey," I nod.

He swallows hard. "This is weird. I don't know anyone here. I've only met the groom at work a couple of times. Don't know why he invited me, but I couldn't turn him down."

"Relax. I'm Sam, and this is—"

I look back and stop dead.

Karmady's changed. Big time. She's squinting cruelly across the ballroom, radiating sheer hate. Her black aura's heavy, chilling me to the bone.

Nervous-Guy looks away, too worried about himself to notice. Forgetting him, I follow her gaze to a group of men at a table. They're laughing loudly, lapping it up.

I turn back to her and ask, "Everything okay?"

She speaks icily. "Soon will be, dude."

I look at them again. They're in fits. Their laughter bellows over the ballroom, then the big man in the middle starts coughing. A small cough at first, which grows steadily louder. Harder. The laughter falls. Quips and jokes are made at his expense as concerned looks from the other guests grow.

The coughing grows severe.

A woman rises from her table and steps in, giving him a glass of water. He takes a sip. It doesn't help. He struggles up from his seat, rounds the table, reaches the ballroom doors, enters the corridor, and hurries off.

Murmurs follow.

A man from the table makes a quip. Nervous laughter rises. No one goes after him.

"Bastards," I murmur. "They should check if he's okay."

I turn to Karmady. She's smugly taking a sip of wine, satisfied. She's loving every second. Her contempt's obvious. Disgustingly so.

The wedding reception goes back into full swing, like nothing's happened. The waiters, the hotel staff, the guests, no one's checking on him. They're all enjoying themselves too much to care. What the hell, I wonder? A guy hurks his guts up, runs out and nobody bats an eyelid. Even the woman who offered him water's gone back to her seat. This is all wrong. Dead wrong.

Enough's enough.

I move to stand. "I'll be right back …"

Karmady's hand snaps up, grabbing my arm. Her touch is prickling. She speaks coldly. "Sit down. Dinner's on its way." Her tone darkens. "It's steak. You like steak. Steak and potatoes. Nice, juicy potatoes. They're your favourite."

How the hell does she know that?

Her gaze bores into me. "Stick around, man. We don't want a missed steak now, do we?"

She's freaking me out. I know she's set the whole thing up. God knows how, but I'm sure of it. Staying here won't help anyone, least of all Coughing-Guy.

She nods to the waiter bringing a tray of food in. "You're steak's almost here."

I ignore her, making no bones about it. "Cut the bull. I'm off."

I head away.

I reach the entrance, moving past a mirror. A glance shows her face in it. A shimmering black halo's engulfed her. Or is it the light? Whatever. A sick guy needs my help and fast. I don't know what the hell's going on but I'm the only one who can save him.

Defying her cold stare, I hurry from the room.

I hear his coughing from miles away. His loud hacking's cringeworthy. I look down the lavish staircase to find it erupting from the bathroom at the bottom. No one's running in. The ushers and passers-by are carrying on as normal.

Moving quickly, I hurry down the steps and reach the ground floor, passing a display cabinet of antique swords. His coughs grow harsh. Excruciating as he desperately fights for the oxygen he needs.

I brace myself, push the bathroom door in and enter. He's leaning over the basin as his chest heaves, like he's trying to hurk up a huge vomit blob. His phone's by his hand. Unlocked. I grab it, ready to call an ambulance.

He raises his head and looks at me pleadingly, his eyes bulging out of their sockets. I gaze back in shock, before he lurches over the sink again, coughing harder and harder. I watch, sickened as he suddenly rises, arches up with a gasping choke and then…

Thuk!

A small, black object flies from his throat, hitting the sink. I jump, expecting to see a thick chunk of bodily fluid.

Instead, it's a large black marble.

I watch, confused, as it rolls around the basin loudly, before resting in the plughole.

Silence follows.

I stare at it, astonished, then look back at him. He turns to me as his mouth opens in a silent scream. I recoil, dropping the phone which smashes to the floor, breaking the screen and dying. Just like him, it seems.

He closes in with staggering steps, clasps my wrist, and stares into my eyes, terrified. His grip tightens, then suddenly loosens as he staggers back, hits the wall and drops to the floor. His head strikes the tiles with a sickening crack, rises a little and smacks down hard. I lean in, reach for him and then …

Bang!

His whole body explodes.

A wave of red mucous, bones and bodily organs burst up like a giant, bloodied firework. I fly back as the outpouring splatters everywhere. The mirror, sink, toilet doors, the carpet, the whole lot drenches in his fleshy remains.

And worst of all, me.

The blood slops over me as I hit the wall with a cry, feeling the thick red patches drizzle over my cheeks, nose and mouth in a sheer nightmare of bloody hell. Heavy dollops drop from my eyes as I see what's left of him liquify, splatter to the floor and trickle for the drain. I'm ready to heave, praying that I won't go the same way when …

A black mist wafts from the sink, rising from the marble he's hurked up. Steadily, it forms into a mass of dark tendrils, reaching in and touching everything in sight. Bit by bit, they absorb the recesses of his foul remains. I cringe as the chilling mist sweeps in, prickling my skin and then engulfing me in a foul shower that feels feral but … cleansing.

Startled, I watch as the blood, organs and the rest of his insides slowly disappear from the room, along with the crap I'm drenched in. Every particle's drawn into the mist, only to drain down its tendrils and back into the marble.

My gaze turns to the mirror, watching in awe, as my face clears of putrid bodily grime and the blood fades from my clothes which smooth neatly over my body, without a crease. My hair tidies itself up, leaving no strand out of place, while my skin clears off his remains, growing spotless. I hold up my hands, seeing the blood upon them vanish, in what can only be described as a bloody miracle.

Bewildered, I watch the unholy cloud retract into the black marble in a massive hell-suck. Twisting, churning and gaining speed in its descent, the mist swoops in until the last wisp shoots inside, making the marble roll a little in the plughole.

Leaving a pristine perfect bathroom.

I look around, astounded, and run a hand through my perfectly combed hair. There's nothing left. No sign he was ever here. Even his phone's vanished. All traces of him are gone.

Except for one thing.

Warily, I walk over to the sink and peer inside.

The black marble's still there.

I swallow hard, longing to know the truth. I can't be nuts. This isn't just me, I'm sure of it. No, I'm being screwed over, just like Marble-Guy who's gone from one ballroom to another.

Fighting against my better nature, I reach for the marble. Carefully, I pick it up, clutching it tightly.

The icy orb tingles in my touch, like it's alive. Marble-Guy had clasped my arm before being blown into hell. Now I sense his presence vividly. No. More than that. His life force.

The bathroom door opens, making me jump.

A man enters.

"Great party, huh?" he says, walking in.

"Yeah," I reply, popping the marble into my pocket while glancing at the floor where the body exploded. "It's … um … gone off with a bang."

He grins. "The best is yet to come."

Unnerved, I head out the door and into the foyer, wondering what to do next, then stop dead.

An ugly thought arises.

I could have gone the same way as Marble-Guy, I conclude, but no. I've been kept alive for a reason. If I keep the marble and run, I'll be a target. Same if I ditch it and go. I'm screwed either way.

My hand wraps over my pocket. The marble tingles inside.

The answer, it seems, lies hidden in the ballroom.

I head for the stairs.

One thing's for sure, I conclude, the Karmady around here's no laughing matter.

The wedding reception's in full swing. Dinner's been served and every-one's tucking in. Otherwise, nothing's changed in the slightest.

Karmady's absorbed in her dinner. I start walking over, then stop by the table where Marble-Guy had been sitting. I look at the place cards. There's no sign of his, as expected. Even worse, his buddies are still laughing their heads off.

One looks up at me. "Oi, oi, lads. Security's here. Look away fella's. Think he's ready to flash his badge."

"You wish," I retort.

The laughter lowers and a deep "Oooooooh …" goes over the table.

I nod at Marble-Guy's empty chair. "Forget it. I'm just looking for some-one."

The main guy glances at it. "Who? The invisible man? Makes no difference to me mate, I'm already blind drunk!"

They crack up again.

Another man cuts in. "Hey, our missing bloke probably went to the bath-room. Like this guy here, he's taking the …"

Bellowing howls erupt from the table as it's banged heartily.

The first man wipes his eyes and says. "You're worse than me, mate." He points at the empty space, looks at me and says, "No card here, but do you want to see mine? I've got plenty." He pulls out his wallet, opens it and starts flicking through. "Oh no, not that one. The cops gave it to me. Says I'm not to go near anyone on a mine site. It wasn't my fault. I was at one when this bird came up and said she wanted to show me her passages."

The laughter explodes again.

"The cops didn't believe me," he says, struggling through chuckles. "Even when I told 'em that she loved nothing better than going up and down a shaft."

They all burst into hysterics.

"Did she … did she … pinch your nuggets?" another man cries.

The man next to him starts banging the table.

I sigh wearily and turn away. "She probably pinched your brain."

They ignore me and howl drunkenly on.

I look ahead. Karmady's still in her spot, tucking heartily into a sausage. She's by herself now. Shy-Guy's shot off somewhere.

I make my way over, reaching the table.

"Oghf!" she says, loving her food. "There's nothing like a nice, juicy banger, is there? Love it."

I draw a sharp breath, lean over her, put one hand on the back of her chair and the other on the table.

"What's the story?" I ask darkly.

She keeps eating.

I press on. "The big guy who was sitting over there. Talk."

She swallows her mouthful and goes for another bite.

I reach into my pocket, pull out the black marble and hold it before her. "Guess this is mine then."

Her face hardens. She goes to grab it.

I pull it back.

"Gimme that!" she hisses.

"Why?" I ask.

Her tone lowers. "You saw how he ended up, right?"

I relent and flick the marble up. She opens her handbag, letting it drop right in. She snaps it closed, smiles happily, picks up her fork and resumes eating. "Thanks man. Oh, this is good."

I sit next to her.

"Glad you came back," she says.

"No choice," I answer. "Stay or run, I'm screwed either way."

She flicks a glance at the wine list. "So order a screwdriver."

I look at her curiously. Realisation hits. "Are you even on the guest list?"

She holds a hand up. "Uh, you have *no* say in this." She gets ready to stab her sausage.

I pull the plate away. "Seriously?"

"Bad move," she warns.

"Answers," I press.

She sighs, putting her fork down. "Don't push it. That's how it starts. Marble-Guy riled who I work for. He made them blow, so they did the same to him. Now give me back my damn food."

42

"Or what?" I counter. "I'll go the same way? Who's your boss? Must be one hell of a business."

She looks away, takes a deep breath, then looks back. "All right hotshot, I'll tell you. For a price."

"Always a catch, isn't there?"

"Happens when you throw yourself into things."

I glance at her bag. "And you've got the balls to kick things off?"

She motions to her glass. "A drink first. You can pay for the rest later."

"Not sure if I can afford it after that drink."

"Not sure if you can afford not to."

"If things are this big, I must be in Texas."

"Take on my Boss and you'll be in a different state by sun-up. Now get me my drink. God knows I want to be in another state too."

I call the waiter over. He takes a drink from his tray, puts it before us, and leaves.

She takes a sip. "Not bad. Unlike some."

I look around. "You have your drink and I'm left clutching at straws. Spill."

"I'm a Debt Collector," she says straight up.

I frown, taking this in. "For who?"

"A firm," she answers. "Makes me a Firm Hand. They give me a job, I go do it. Simple."

"Going by what I've seen, you must get your jobs telepathically."

She taps her head. "Oh yeah, I'm the Karmady Channel."

"You're sure cracking me up."

She shrugs. "I get paid well for it. Real well. I'm laughing all the way to the bank."

"Now I know you're a joke."

"Hey, Marble-Guy got what was coming to him. Three weeks ago he got drunk and beat up a guy near a nightclub. Guy later died, screwing up a bigger operation for the Boss and leaving our Firm ... unbalanced. Marble-Guy's debt went into the blood red, and now ..." she taps her bag with the marble inside "... he's back in the black. Nothing like a nice round figure."

I shake my head, disgusted. "So what's that? His in-voice?"

She smirks. "Lighten up, dude. When you don't your bad vibes crystallise and then ..." She opens her bag, showing the marble "... your balls drop off."

I avert my gaze, sickened. "Cut the crap. You're here, your Boss isn't, and there's a dead guy, thanks to *you*."

She glances across the room. "Who says I'm alone? See the girl in red over there?"

I follow her gaze. A brunette's at the far table, looking into her purse and counting a mass of notes.

I nod, impressed. "How can I miss her with that figure?"

"Then there's Moustache-Guy two tables to the right," she continues. "A couple of guys outside too. Big op's going down tonight and you're the tool who's thrown himself into the works. You shouldn't even know this much."

I draw a sharp breath. "Hey, I'm involved now, so I'm a target too. Right?"

She shrugs. "There are more targets, yeah."

"That's not a damn answer."

"I'm not paid to give a damn."

I tense, not liking this one bit. "But the Firm won't let me go. Will it?"

Silence.

"Will it?"

More silence.

Her phone beeps on the table. "Oh!" She looks at the message and puts it in her bag. "Gotta go." She rises quickly, straps her bag over her shoulder, picks up her coat and says, "Hell hath no fury like a woman possessed."

"Let me guess," I say. "Your target?"

"Everyone's got a price to pay, man."

"So why not do it from here?" I press. "Like when you cut Marble-Guy down to size?"

She slaps my shoulder. "This one's on special offer. Bye." She hurries away.

I watch as she heads past Red-Dress Girl who's typing into her phone. Red-Dress buzzed Karmady, I can tell. Red-Dress puts it down and we both watch Karmady head across the room. Straight for …

My heart stops.

A boy. About ten years old. He's coughing hard. Even worse, he's risen from his chair, making for the door.

I shudder. This is wrong, so wrong. Whatever this kid's done, however bad, she can't take the life of a child. No way. She's already crossed the line by killing Marble-Guy. Now she's damn obliterating it.

I leap out of my chair and hurry after them, concerned for the kid and vowing to end this crap here and now. Like before, nobody else is giving a damn. They're too absorbed in clasping their own cocktails.

The kid's way ahead of Karmady who's way ahead of me. He stumbles into the foyer and staggers down the lavish staircase. She follows, albeit at a distance. I reach the foyer just as he hits the ground floor, flails sickeningly ahead, thuds into the bathroom door and lurches inside.

She passes a mirror. I catch a glimpse of her face in it. She's squinting evilly, spitting out curses of sheer hate. He staggers into the bathroom, gasping for air. She raises her arm, pushes the door open and strides in.

I sweep down the staircase, thinking rapidly. There's got to be a way to save him. I can't let a kid die. A *kid* for god's sake. Doing nothing makes me just as much of a killer. There's no choice. It's lose-lose.

I hit the floor, stumble, and grab the glass cabinet for balance. It wobbles slightly, shaking the swords inside.

Locked. As expected.

A wail erupts from the bathroom.

Enough's enough. It's either her, me or the kid.

I run to the opposite wall, grab a wooden chair and surge furiously at the cabinet.

Bang!

The chair slams in hard, its heavy impact cracking the glass. I smash it again and again. A man yells from the top of the stairs, then runs to get help. I ignore him and keep smashing the glass. A couple more blows make a hole big enough to reach through. I flip the chair around, use its leg to clear the glass, then reach in and grab a ceremonial sword. A shard of glass cuts the back of my hand. It's not deep but stings like hell. Red droplets fall on the blade as I pull the sword out.

A security guard yells from the top of the stairs.

Forgetting him, I lunge at the bathroom door, bursting through it. The boy's by the sink, his head lowered. Karmady stands nearby, looming over him.

Now or never.

I raise the sword with a cry, ready to rip into her.

She turns to me, unfazed, and smirks. Worse still, the boy stops coughing. He stands smoothly to face me, grinning cockily.

I freeze in horror.

He's fine. Worse than fine. On top of a sick game.

The truth hits me hard. The whole thing's a setup. For me.

"Crapp-in-hell!"

I lower the sword in shock.

She steps in. "Hey, just knowing about us incurs a debt, man. Gotta pay up. With twenty pieces of ..." She smirks "... Silver."

My mind whirrs. Despite the horror, there's so many questions. I'm not letting this go. I can't.

"Why the set-up with you and the kid?" I press. "Why not talk upstairs?"

Crash!

I jump, knowing that the sword cabinet outside's toppled over. The guard's cry follows from under it.

Karmady's work. That's obvious.

My throat tingles. A lump's forming. Round. Crystallised. Growing hot as it expands. I cough, then feel it stop, retracting a little. Hovering between the stages of its inhuman growth.

"I get it," I whisper. "You're sucking me in." Realisation dawns as I feel the lump rising and falling. "For a job." I shiver as the truth hits home. "Marble-Guy was my induction."

She grins. "Hey, I like what I see. You can make a real killing here."

"At a high price," I counter.

"Special offer," she states. "When guard-boy out there flies in and sees you holding a sword on me and the kid it aint gonna look good. 'Course I can fix that. No one knows about Marble-Guy now so I can change his mind ... literally. Sign up with us and he'll forget the whole thing."

The marble expands in my throat.

She pushes on. "Say no and we'll take you by the balls. Yes or no, Silver."

I hear the cabinet outside rise loudly. A groan follows as the Guard shuffles out.

I draw a sharp breath. "So I'm either siding with you or stoned forever? Get stuffed, neither's living."

"Last chance ..." she presses.

"No chance," I shoot back, raising the sword. "Forget it!"

The door bursts open and the guard sweeps in, ready to fire.

The marble expands rapidly in my throat.

I whirl around hysterically, slashing hard. He howls as the sword slices across his chest, then falls wailing. Caught in the momentum, I swirl back, lunging at the boy. He dodges the blade, letting it sweep dangerously past his head and hit the sink. Choking horrifically, I raise the sword again and slash back at Karmady. A glance in the mirror shows the Guard hitting the floor, his arm flying up with the gun and then …

Bang!

The blade slices through Karmady and the bullet thuds into my back, firing me from reality.

I drop the pages not believing a word. Taking a deep breath, I sit up against the wall, then glimpse at the back of my hand. Slowly, I raise it, turning it over. A long scab's zigzagging over my skin, filled with dark, dried blood.

My gaze lowers to the floor where the fallen story lies. Part of it's facing upwards. I read what's on it.

A shard of glass cuts the back of my hand. It's not deep but stings like hell. Red droplets fall on the blade as I pull the sword out.

I raise my other hand, running it gingerly over the cut.

My head swirls. Logically, this can't be the true story. A paranormal firm making those in debt cough up black marbles and then explode? People wiped from existence? Reality bent to hell? How can this garbage be real?

Then again, look where I am. No memory, a dead body, six stories and a psychotic voice that may or may not be in my head.

I look around, blinking hazily. Sure, this could be a Firm Hand training ground but no, that's unlikely. Operating like this makes no sense, even for them. They're way too strong. Maybe Karmady's gone rogue and wants revenge, but there's no evidence for that either. I won't delve into fantasy scenarios. That'll only drive me insane, if I'm not already.

I rub my back. No gunshot wound there, so that's good. Whether the story's real or not, I have it for a reason. Why?

Further stories will tell.

I pick up the next one.

Evolutionary Road.

I swear under my breath, sensing that this'll be *more* way out.

I brace myself and read aloud.

Chapter Three

Evolutionary Road

Nature always comes out on top.

Grey clouds loom in the distance. I see them from my study window, dismayed. I *so* want to go for a walk. No, scratch that, I *need* a walk, but a storm's coming. Figures. I finish my latest novel after several hours of a writing binge and what do I get? Stuck in the house because of rain.

Stuff it, I'll take the risk. The clouds look bad, sure, but the weather guys usually get it wrong. Hopefully, there might only be a drizzle. Whatever happens, I have to get out of the house and fast. I'll go nuts otherwise. That's the price for being a lonely writer.

I grab a jacket with a hood and head off. The phone stays at home. I never take it on walks. After countless screen edits I can't bear the thought of seeing anything but real life.

The walk starts okay, despite the looming clouds. They're way off but moving in fast, growing darker by the moment. I quicken my pace, hoping to get a short walk in before the downpour. It won't be much, but'll help.

It's the usual trip. Across the road, through the park, a short walk along a narrow street, down the slope and into the bushland. A gravel path'll lead me to the school, then it's a sharp U-turn and back the way I came.

I make it to the bushland and onto the dusty track. The path's wide enough for people and bikes to pass each other easily, while the main road's nearby, running parallel to the bushland.

The cool breeze suddenly changes as a warm wind picks up. Dizziness hits. The world swirls and I stop and blink. For a second, just a second, my mind tingles, tinged by a wave of nausea. Luckily, it passes just as fast. I blink again. It's probably nothing, I figure. A penalty for my writing binge. I shake it off and move on.

My head tingles with the nausea's residue as I walk further along the path. The warm breeze picks up and the tingling grows, as does my paranoia. I feel … watched. Studied. Scrutinised. Like someone's behind me, looking over my shoulder. Swamping me like the wind.

My dread grows.

I turn and look back.

Nothing.

A lump forms in my throat. I'm creeped out. I don't know why. No, this isn't just the writing binge.

The nearby bushes rustle loudly.

I jump.

Must be an animal or bird in there. Sounds big too. At least it's staying put, thank god, but I'm outta here.

I hurry along.

The sky rumbles. Great, that's just what I need. The storm's come early. Good thing is, the school's up ahead and I need cover.

I take a few more steps, then stop. A grotesque magpie's perched on a dead tree branch, glaring at me, like I'm transparent. I freeze, feeling like a worm, while staring back at its misshapen head and crooked beak. We watch each other, our gazes locked as the tension mounts, each daring the other to make the first move. This deformed beast's got the upper hand, for its confidence far outstrips mine.

Splash!

An icy raindrop hits my eye.

I blink.

The magpie screeches, leaps and swoops. I duck as it flies over my head, soars high and whirls around. Freaked out, I rise and stumble away. Another screech follows as it swoops again, ready for a vicious stab at my temple.

I turn back, stumble and plummet into the gravel, hitting my head. A flash erupts behind my eyes as I tumble down a slope. The world blurs in a kaleidoscope of colours as I plummet for the lone bush below, leaving the hellbird sweeping over.

Branches scratch my face. Bones crack and creak louder than I ever thought possible, twisting into places they shouldn't, while muscles I never knew I had stretch to extreme lengths. I cry out as I roll into the bush, entering its dark embrace.

Snap!

A thick cluster of branches brings me to a sudden stop.

My face is riddled with cuts. My body with scratches. Blood wells under my skin, ready to form massive bruises. I ache all over from the fall, but it doesn't feel like anything's broken. Physically, I'm not too bad. Otherwise, I'm a damn mess.

Rustling comes from above. I peer through the branches, seeing the magpie land on a tree stump at the slope's peak. Its ugly head perks about, looking for me. I hold my breath, watching the hell-bird. Finally, it tenses, leaps, and flies off.

I sigh gratefully and push myself up.

My hand slips and falls, dropping into an open space. I look down. There's a large hole, possibly a burrow, partially covered with roots. Maybe big enough for a dwarf to fit through. The dirt's disturbed, like a creature's just scuttled in. Another reason to ditch this place fast.

I pull my hand out, inch away, then stop dead.

A long, black snake's slithering out from the dark opening.

My heart pounds. I gaze at it in shock, watching as the hideous reptile slides over my hand. I grimace sickly as it touches my fingers, slipping over my arm and then sliding onto my stomach. I hold my breath, keeping deathly still, trying not to explode. I watch, terrified, as it curls up and settles on my chest, its hot tongue hissing near my face. Like the magpie, it's squinting deep into my eyes, observing me. It too is conscious, knowing me inside out, while daring me to make the first move.

I stare at it horrified. Fighting's not an option. Nor is waiting it out. I can't stay here, but I need to do something. I need ...

'*Ramble, ramble, ramble ...*'

The murky voice chills me to the bone. A voice not in my head, but from the burrow. Its tone rises, like its singing, then morphs into cackles of sick delight.

What's more, it sounds human.

Almost human.

The cackling closes in, growing darker. Slimier. Louder. Shifting between insane gurgles and sobs of anguish. Scratchy words, like that of a crackly old crone, follow. I shudder as the grizzling warbles leach through my ears, drilling into my brain.

'*Ramble, ramble, ramble ...*'

''*Goblins ...*'

'*Minnows ...*'

'*Pond scum ...*'

Scratching shuffles come from the hole.

It's close now. So close.

Panic takes over.

My hand flashes up, grabbing the snake by the neck and hurling it into the hole. Taken by surprise, the snake flails into the darkness, before a massive shriek erupts, like whatever's in there's bitten.

My body shoots into overdrive. Searing daggers of pain ripple through me amid the rising tide of nausea, dizziness and terror. I push it aside, scrambling out of the bush and up the slope. I barely reach the path when another icy droplet hits my face.

More drops follow, along with a vicious thunderclap. A fierce caw comes from above before the hideously deformed magpie swoops in again. I duck in pure agony. The risk pays off and the bird sweeps over my head once more. Enraged by this crap, seething with an anger I never knew I had, I grab a rock, hurling it high with pure hate. The rock soars through the air and ...

Thuk!

The bird's hit square on. Both it and the rock plummet, hitting the ground hard. The rock rolls away while the magpie twitches, blood streaming from its head. I shudder, not knowing what's worse. The horror inside me, or this damn place.

I rise again, my pain dispelling my rage. The bush below rustles fiercely, filled with the creature's insane ranting, like it's ready to burst out. Ignoring it, I stumble away, skidding down a gravel path and reaching a small, wooden bridge. Achingly, I cross it, coming to a wooden staircase, rising to the main road.

I skid again but keep going, glancing back to see waves of bushes rustling heavily as the shrieking '*Rambler*' runs through them, chasing me.

I scramble up the wooden staircase. Every step's horrendous. My ankles kill and my dizziness grows. The thunder bellows amid bucketing torrents of rain, soaking me to the bone. A fierce wind sweeps in, striking me hard as I struggle to reach the peak. A manic burst of strength brings me to the top. Blind panic follows as I stagger onto the main road.

A wailing horn erupts. I leap sideways as a truck rushes by, sending a furious burst of water flying high, drenching me. Ignoring the danger, I run in front of another wailing car before reaching the island in the middle of the road. Streams of cars drive past on either side as the drivers glance at me strangely. I don't care. I'm just glad they can see me.

A large shrub by the wooden staircase rustles loudly. Despite the storm and the cars sweeping by, the wind carries the distant, crackly *'Ramble, ramble, ramble'* coming from the slope's peak. The creature, I now call the Rambler, screeches, then fades, retreating into the bushland.

Sighing wearily, I collapse to the ground.

I'm safe.

For now.

The walk home's chilling. I limp along, sticking to the main road in clear sight of the cars. I'm cut, bloodied and bruised, but nobody pulls over, nor cares, only wanting to shoot off as fast as possible. My mind races as I plough through the storm. Is the Rambler even real? Or am I insane? Right now, it's too hard to tell.

My house isn't far, but a little too close to the bushland for my liking. I should go to the shops and get help, maybe use their phone, but there'd be too many questions. I need time to think. Home's closer anyway. Trouble is, my car's being fixed at the garage, so there's no chance of leaving the house. If I get inside and lock the doors, I should be okay. I'll make up a story, call a friend and have them pick me up. Shouldn't be a problem, I'm a writer after all. I can spend the night at their place and then figure out what to do next. No, home's the safest bet for now. I'm sure of it.

I reach my house none too soon. It feels like a lifetime since I've left. My hands fumble as I grab the keys, unlock the door, dive inside and slam it shut behind me, bolting it tightly. A lightning flash fills the darkness as the roaring thunder shakes the walls. I hit the light switch. Nothing. I try it again, then again. Still nothing. Power's out.

My heart pounds. If the power's gone then …

I hobble to the table and grab my mobile. It's dead. I'd left it on charge before heading off. The power must have gone out shortly after. Even worse, no power means the landline'll also be dead. This is bad. No choice now but to risk it. I'll have to see my neighbours. God knows what I'll tell them, but if–

'Ramble, ramble, ramble ...'

Soft shuffling outside chills me to the bone. Gurgles grow as the sick voice rises with mumbles, mutters and sniffs. Cries and wails grow over the storm. Loneliness, despair and madness all rolled into one.

I freeze, then slowly inch back, pushing myself up against the wall, not daring to move. What the hell is this, a breakdown? Writing for so long today could have done it. The storm's playing tricks on me. It must be.

I barely notice the creaks in the gutter, then the roof, then ...

Slam!

The bathroom door.

I jump with a lightning flash, terrified. Desperately, I cower behind the lounge chair, my mind ablaze. No, this can't be real. No way. I always leave my bathroom window a quarter open but locked. A wind gust must have swept through, slamming the door shut. That's it. Please God, let it be it.

A scratchy voice rises from down the hallway.

'Ramble, ramble, ramble ...'

My heart jolts.

The Rambler's here. In my damn house.

The floorboards creak under its weight. It's crackly voice etches into my brain, singing softly.

'Coming home, coming home ...'

I bite my lip and clench my fist, trying not to scream. Tears well in my eyes as the Rambler closes in, shuffling along the hallway for the lounge. I can't lunge for the front door. It's locked. I'm Rambler food if I try.

I crouch in the shadows, curling up, not daring to breathe.

'Ramble, ramble, ramble...'

Sloppy wet footsteps enter the lounge, squelching over the carpet. I peer sideways. Two stubby, slimy feet are in the shadows. Jet black. Oozing with dripping muck.

'Ramble, ramble, ramble ...'

A muddy flapper rises.

Hysteria explodes and I leap up, hoisting the couch over in a maniacal frenzy, dumping it on the Rambler. The dwarf screeches, vanishing under it as I turn and fly down the hallway, ignoring my body's throbbing, searing agony.

I run into the laundry, making for the back door.

Thud!

I hear the couch flip over, hitting the floor. Another screech erupts. My hand snaps up, grabbing the door handle. It turns easily, already open. That must be how the Rambler got in. God knows how. I locked it before leaving for that damn walk I never should have started.

Soft, light footsteps run across the floorboards, heading for the laundry.

I wrench the door open and run outside, into the raging storm. The freezing rain gushes over me as I hobble past the clothesline, around the shed and into the backyard. An owl hoots from a tree. A loud flutter and a sweeping rush follow. I look up, then duck as the owl flies over my head, wailing loudly.

Clank!

I glance at the kitchen. The dwarf's in my living room, heading for the backdoor. I ignore it and push on, making for the carport, growing slower with every step. Finally, I reach the front gate. It too is open. I stumble past it, fleeing through the carport and onto my driveway. I have to reach my neighbours. They're the only ones who can help. My last resort. They're …

Not home.

Like me, they don't have a garage door and there's no sign of the car.

A bellowing howl erupts. I look up the driveway and stop dead. A wild dog's poised in the rain, panting hungrily, saliva dripping from its jaw. It snarls, ready to pounce.

The owl swoops again and I recoil, dropping onto the driveway. Feathers rustle as it lands on my bin, watching me closely, just like the dog.

A steady stream of ants rise from a concrete crack, struggling against the rain. Many are swept away. The rest press on, despite the mounting odds. Slugs, snails and spiders emerge from the garden, along with insects so alien I could hurl. Why the hell are they crawling out into the storm, gunning for me, along with the owl and the hellhound? What's the damn point? Why do this? Why …?

Realisation strikes like a thunderbolt.

Nature! Whatever the Rambler is, it controls nature!

I start to rise.

The dog's faster, surging in, leaping high and thudding into me. We hit the ground hard as its claws dig into my chest. I struggle back as its long saliva streams drip hungrily over my cheeks.

I don't have a chance.

The owl perks its head sideways, listening closely, then watches the front door eerily creak open. Short, shuffling, footsteps approach, splashing through the deepening puddles.

'Ramble, ramble, ramble...'

They draw closer. A slimy, oozing flapper touches my face.

I scream ...

***

My eyes flicker open.

Sunlight streams through a gap in my blinds.

I'm in bed. The storm's passed. The sun's out. The neighbours are working in the garden, talking happily. A bird's perched on my fence, singing. Another joins in. Everything's cruisy, as usual, but ...

A gaping gap's in my mind. No, more than that. A massive black hole. I frown, trying to work it out. Nothing, nothing, nothing and then ...

Flash!

Last night's horror ignites like a firework, blowing my mind. I shoot up like an arrow. My arms press firmly against the bed as my heart pounds, ready to burst from my chest. Terror sweeps in like a hurricane. The dog, the owl, the snake, the magpie, the bush, the *Rambler!* Piercing visions slice my mind as hysteria mounts. God, I'm having a breakdown! I have to be! Physically, I feel fine. There's no pain. No injuries. My room's spotless, as usual, so why the freak out? What the hell?

Squelch!

I freeze in terror, then slowly look down.

Thick, black, oozy slime's drenched my bed, soaking it.

Instinctively, I raise my hand.

It's not there.

Only a thick, black, leathery flipper.

I scream. Or at least try to. A high-pitched squeal erupts as I roll over and drop out of bed, splashing heavily onto the floor. My body's shorter. Wider. Like a dwarf.

I push myself up. Panic hits. I try to run. Thick, heavy steps propel me out of my room, thumping along the corridor. The house towers over me. The doors, the walls, the cupboards, all loom high as I thump flabbily past them, entering the bathroom. I'm far too small to see myself in the mirror. Grimacing, I lift a slippery foot onto the bathtub's edge and step up, squashing a black flipper near the sink to steady myself. Slowly, and with great effort, I rise, before slipping forward, squashing slimily onto the sink and facing my reflection head-on. I try screaming again, but what comes out is ...

'Ramble, ramble, ramble ...'

I recoil in horror, plummet from the sink and hit the tiles with a splattering squelch. Nothing hurts. I'm too rubbery for that. I choke back the nausea as I stare at the distant roof, lying in despair.

I gurgle again. Unlike the Rambler, my tone's lower. Heavier. Deeper. Realisation hits.

The Rambler had been female. I'm sure of it. No doubt human once. Perhaps caught by another Rambler who'd forced her mutation. All she'd been doing was reaching out for help that'd never arrive.

My mind races. Is the Rambler curse cast off when passed to another victim? Or is there a whole host of slimy dwarves in the bush, linked in a bloodied chain of despair?

Whatever. I can't stay here. Someone'll come sooner or later. Friends. Family. Neighbours. Who cares? I'm screwed if they do. I have to leave and fast. To go into hiding, then find answers.

I'll lie low and wait for night to come. When the shadows fall and the moon rises, I'll start what I didn't finish.

A walk in the bush. The ultimate trek along a new path of an evolutionary road.

Yes, I realise, looking sorrowfully up through the window at the thick grey clouds above, nature always comes out on top.

"What the hell …?"

I lower the pages, frowning. What the crap am I s'posed to learn from this garbage? That I've evolved into a slimeball cousin of a donkey's infected butt, making an ass of myself? Is that it?

I look up at Meridian's speaker. Their Oracle. Yes, I conclude. Meridian's Oracle. Their MO.

Seriously baffled, I say, "I don't get it. What's the story?"

The speaker crackles loudly, then Meridian's dark tone rises. *"What's YOUR story?"* A pause. *"It's waiting."*

The door shakes from an outside breeze. The breeze blows under it, flowing over the floor and rustling the next story, like a creepy prompt.

I look at the body by the desk. My mind races. Paranoia sinks in, filling me with dread. "So what? You want me to think that I wrote too much, had a breakdown, went into the bush and killed this guy, turning me into a monster. Is that it?"

No response.

I rub my temples and glance at the body. "No. You're putting me in the picture by framing me as a killer, but you're forgetting one thing. You said it yourself. This is my story. Not yours."

The voice speaks cruelly. *"So take your story back. You won't get anywhere otherwise. Besides …"* The breeze blows a sheet up, flying past my hand *"… The ending's still up for grabs."*

I snatch the sheet out of the air.

"Very good," Meridian finishes. *"Best not to jump to conclusions."*

"Up yours," I shoot back.

Sighing, I relent, looking at the page. I have to give in. For now. That means wading through Meridian's septic crap and not being dragged under. I need answers. Reading's the only way ahead. I've got no choice,

I sit down and pick up the next pile. I hope to hell it won't be more surreal.

A dark inkling says my hopes'll be in vain.

Chapter Four

Galakir

'Clip, clip, clip …'

The cutters snip fast. Too fast. My neighbour's having a field day with her hedge. I hear her from my deck chair as I sit writing by my fence, old school, with a pen and paper. I'm struggling with the story and the cutters are loud. Distracting. My head's full and they're inflaming my headache. I've had lots lately. Dizziness. Blurred vision. I've been to the doctor and he can't explain it. No tests can pick anything up, freaking me out.

I stand to go inside.

"*Arrrrgggghhh …!*"

The cry's sharp. Stabbing. Like my neighbour's cut herself.

I cringe, knowing her husband's away on business. I hate this. No one's around and I'll have to help. She's getting on and I can't leave her. I toss my pad and pen onto the chair, hurry to the fence, step on a stone pot, and look over.

She's stopped snipping. She's sitting on her knees, gazing around dreamily. There's no sign of blood. She speaks in a high tone, her voice, childlike. "Pep-per-mint …"

There's a potted peppermint plant nearby.

She continues, curiously. "Pep-per-mint … pink. Pep-per-mint in the … pink … pot…" She struggles to get the last word out "… plant."

She blinks hard.

This is nuts. Bracing myself, I say, "Mrs. Turner?"

Her head turns slowly to me. Our eyes meet, chilling me to the bone. This isn't her. She's too far gone for that.

"Who?" she asks innocently.

I turn to go. "I'll be back–"

"No!" she cries. "Don't go–" She tenses "Sam!"

I stop dead. "What? What did you say?"

She shuts her eyes tightly, struggling to think. "I need … to tell you–" She hesitates.

I tense. "Tell me what?"

Her eyes open. "You're … special."

I shake my head. "You need help …"

"We all do," she cuts in, looking at the sky.

"You're telling me …" I begin, wanting to call an ambulance.

"He's back!" she suddenly cries.

I frown. Are we getting somewhere? Has she been hurt in the past? Physically? I need to play along.

"Who?" I ask.

She shivers. "We don't have long."

"I don't …"

Her eyes widen and she gasps, looking around, terrified. "He knows I'm here …!"

I nod, knowing she's nuts. "Stay right there Mrs. Turner–"

She clasps her temples, wincing. "No. Crystal! Crystal … Spinner!" Her head arches back. "Find me …!"

Her mouth opens wide, exhaling a golden mist from her lips. Twisting. Turning. Rising rapidly. It widens, then thins, before shooting over the opposite fence, dropping out of sight.

I gulp, staring at her in shock.

"What the hell are you doing?"

I jump at her harshness. It's Mrs. Turner. The *real* Mrs. Turner. Her cranky self that you never dare mess with. She rises, staring at me crossly.

"Uh …" I begin.

"What do you want?" she huffs.

"I … I …"

"Nothing," she concludes. "Stop spying and go! Now!"

I keep staring at her.

"*Now!*" she bellows.

I jump. "Yeah … uh … sorry." I turn away, step down from the pot and hurry into the house. I shut the door, lean on the wall and think hard. If she's not nuts, I am. My doctor's missed something big. God, I could be dying of a brain disease. That must be it. I'm going crazy, but … no. That doesn't seem right. Physically, I feel normal. Logical. Rational. Sure, there's a little dizziness, but that's all. That leaves three outcomes. I'm crazy, Mrs. Turner's crazy … or Ghost-Kid's real.

Maybe she is. Maybe not. My headaches could've been her trying to reach me. Whatever. It's useless to speculate. The only option now's to do what she said and find out about her. Crystal Spinner. That means research. If I find anything, great. If not, it's off to the doctor. Again. No, I have to prove she's real, meaning I need answers fast. Chasing this up's the only way.

I go to my study, sit at my PC and hit a button, ready to net-search her name.

Damn. NBN's down.

Worse still, my phone's at the shop, having its screen fixed.

Only one thing for it.

The library.

The library's close by. Only a five-minute walk from my house, so that helps.

I head to a PC. The monitor's off. I reach for a button but the screen flickers, then activates, and the PC logs itself on. Probably an IT guy playing around remotely, I figure.

Or not.

A search engine appears. A link's clicked and a recent article comes up. The screen zeroes in on a photo. A little girl. Blonde-haired, pretty, and peachy perfect. Her name's under it.

Crystal Spinner. Age 10.

I tense, stunned.

The young librarian looks over.

"You okay?" she asks, from behind the desk.

I keep staring at the screen.

"You need help?" she presses.

I turn to her. "No, I'm fine."

She indicates the screen. "IT again. I'll put a sign on it. We'll set you up with another PC."

I hold my hand up. "Hang on, I just want to read that article."

She shrugs. "Go for it." She turns to an old lady.

I sit at the PC. Crystal's face stares back, confirming I'm not nuts. She's seated on a lounge sofa in a lavish room, smiling, with the puerile presence Mrs. Turner had. I grab the mouse and scroll through the article. I vaguely recall hearing about it on the news a while back. A busload of passengers went missing in the hills. Sure, the winding paths there are tricky, but there was no wreckage. Anywhere. Not even after a monster search. The whole bus just vanished, like it was sucked into thin air.

I feel a presence over my shoulder, then look up with a start.

A girl my age stands behind me, staring at the screen. She's similar to Crystal, in the face anyway. Frowning, she catches my gaze, then turns away.

I rise quickly. "Hey, can I ask …?"

She hurries off.

I head after her, following her out of the library, down the steps and into the carpark, running to keep up.

There's only one thing for it.

"Crystal Spinner!" I call.

She stops. I do the same. She turns to face me. Nervously, she pushes strands of her short, dark hair behind her ear. "Sorry, dude. Didn't mean to pry, hey …"

"Forget it," I cut in. "You knew the kid on the screen, right?"

She frowns suspiciously. "Why? Who are you?"

"Sam Silver. I'm a writer."

"So what? You write books on missing kids?"

I give a relieved sigh, knowing she's caught up in this crap too. "Oh, thank god. I'm looking for answers." My mind races. "About that busload of people who went AWOL in the hills. You know anything?"

She glares at me. Her jaw tightens as our eyes meet. Seeing I'm no threat, she submits, albeit reluctantly. "Maybe."

"Can I help?"

"Doubt it." She lets loose with a sigh. "That kid in the shot. She was my sister."

I nod, seeing the resemblance. "Sorry to hear that. Did they ever find her?"

"Nah. Just the bus about a week later. Undamaged, with no bodies."

"Seriously?" I ask. "The article said …"

"Old article, doofus," she cuts in.

I mull on this. "Sounds like whatever sucked up the bus, took everyone and spat it back out again."

I suddenly regret what I've said and expect her to explode.

Instead, she says, "Totally. I thought the same."

I press on. "No one used their phones to call out?"

"Would we be here if they did?" she scoffs.

"Good point. Did they find anything on the bus?"

She purses her lips, looks away, puts her hand under her nose and sniffs, like she's holding back the tears.

"You don't have to—" I begin.

"The doors and windows were sealed shut!" she snaps.

My stomach goes queasy. "God, that's feral." I pause. "So how did they get out? Was any stuff left? Bags and things?"

"No!" she retorts. "All I know is that my sister's gone, the cops can't do anything, and you just want to shake my bacon 'cause you're out for a pork. Well let's get one thing straight. *You're* the pig!"

"Don't be a cow!" I shoot back.

"Ah, cut the bull!"

She tramps across the road, making for the shops.

I give a small smile. I can't resist her spark. Like her sister, she's got magic, only hers is down to earth.

I turn to the library. If she won't help, it's back to the PC.

I barely take a step when an old man turns from the library door, staring at me. His eyes are wide. His face white. Like he's terrified. Normally, I'd think he's a demented weirdo, but not now. A dim halo's over his head. Faded gold. I've seen it before.

Crystal's. Only this time, it's darkening.

He calls in her voice, terrified.

"Run!"

Screech!

A black car races 'round the corner, picks up speed, and heads for library-girl crossing the road.

Her head darts up, frozen.

Instinct takes over. I bolt in and leap, taking the mother of all dives. She cries out as I crash into her and we hit the ground hard, rolling away. The car shoots by, veering down the road, then round the corner, speeding off.

I look down at library-girl. "You okay?"

She smacks my arm. "What do you think? Get off!"

"Sure." I roll away.

She sits up, shaking. "I swear that was for me. I know it was."

I frown, thinking hard. I hadn't taken it in at the time, but halfway through the dive I'd caught a glimpse of the car window. The driver had long dark hair and sunglasses. I'd only seen them side-on, but one thing's for sure.

That was a woman.

I look back at the library. The old man's staring at us in horror, the 'Crystal' spirit now gone.

I swallow hard, looking around.

"I hope there are cameras here," I murmur.

The girl gulps, staring after the car. "Why me? What the hell have I done?"

"We were talking about the bus," I reply. "Guess they didn't like it."

She smacks my arm. "What is this, a conspiracy?"

A voice calls from the library door. "Are you alright?"

Desk-girl.

"Yeah," I reply. "Think so."

She nods. "Saw the whole thing. I'll call security. You'd better stick 'round to make a statement."

"Yeah. Sure."

I rise, helping the girl next to me up.

"Thanks, dude," she says.

"Sam," I reply. "You?"

"Amber," she answers. She winces, rubbing her backside. "I don't know what's worse. You or the car. You're both pains in the ar—"

"Are you right to walk?" I cut in.

"Oh, shut up!"

Now I'm annoyed. "You shut up!"

She smacks me lightly. I smack her back. She smacks me again, pushing me away.

"Move 'em or lose 'em!"

"You two are so matched," Desk-girl calls.

"Shut up!" we both snap at her.

64

She grins and guides us inside.

Security arrives and starts sorting through the outside footage. Amber tells me she's hesitant to show her butt in daylight. I tell her if she shows it at night it'd be a full moon. She smacks me again. This time, I see the faint glimmer of a smile.

With time to kill, I sit at a PC, log in, and scan the net, searching for anything on Crystal Spinner and the bus. Amber joins me, curious to see the article I'd found earlier. Finally, it comes up, showing Crystal once more. Amber takes a seat and cringes. Not just from the photo but her sore butt too.

We scan the article, finding nothing. Amber checks her social media page. No messages. She scrolls down. It's full of family shots. One stands out and she tenses.

Crystal, on a loungeroom sofa, next to a man.

Amber sniffs sadly. "God, I'm almost flattened outside and now I'm being crushed by this." She peers into the screen. "Wait up. Who's that?"

"The guy?"

"What are you blind? The freak watching through the damn window." She zooms in. Her jaw drops and we both gasp, letting loose with a "Whoa!"

A man stands there, looking in. Like Ghost-Crystal, he's got a halo, only his is jet-black. Wavering. Jagged. Distorted. He's tall, about eight feet, wearing jeans and a flannel shirt. His bald head's twisted sideways as he gurns grotesquely, looking like a wounded soldier I saw in the city one night.

Amber shudders. "That's AI. Has to be."

"Aimed at us?" I ask.

"Me," she corrects. "Remember the damn car outside? I'm being gunned for."

"Why? What have you done?"

"Nothing," she snaps back. "Meeting you was my biggest mistake."

I shake my head, loving her spirit, then focus on the screen. There's only three scenarios here. IT. Ghost-Crystal or this … hell-demon.

The screen blurs and, all on its own, brings up the next photo. Crystal and her dad are still on the couch, smiling at the camera, only now hell-demon's in the room, looming behind them.

"Unholy crap!" Amber gasps.

The image blurs again.

He's staring directly ahead.

At us.

No, I realise. At me. Like he knows who I am.

My vision wavers and my head buzzes, like a memory's trying to surface. My hand rises to my temple, then ...

Zip!

Amber's pulled out the PC power cord, killing it.

The world unblurs, I rub my head and sit back shakily.

She trembles. "I seriously thought he was going to jump out of the screen."

"No," I reply. "That was only meant to freak us."

"Like what? A warning shot?"

Realisation dawns. "Oh, you are good! Seriously good."

"I know," she retorts. "Why? You gunning to fork my pork again?"

"Zip it ..."

"I'd love to zip yours."

I press on. "We're targets. I don't know why. Your sister was too, like everyone on the bus. Now it's our turn. Hell's having a party and we're the guests of honour."

She shudders. "Always knew that life was out to get me." She swallows hard. "Even if the shots were fixed, some nutjob still tried flattening me. What's the picture?"

I grin again. "Oh, you're better than good! You're on a roll!"

"If you gun for my buns once more ..."

I push on. "Look, you said *picture*. We just saw a few shots that were messed around with, but there had to be an original. That means ..." My eyes widen " ... a photographer!"

Amber's ready to slap me, then frowns. She raises a finger and says, "Okay, I am good." She pauses. "So that could've been them in the car?"

"Maybe," I reply, knowing she's got part of the truth. Sure, they could've come for us, but that doesn't explain ghost kid, hell-demon, nor the busload of people shooting off to god knows where. Do you remember who took the photo?"

She thinks hard. "Some lady from an agency. Said we'd won a comp."

"You got her details?"

She shakes her head. "No. She didn't stay long. She took snaps of me and my sis in the garden too but ..." She indicates the PC "... I'm not going back into psychoverse to find 'em." She pauses, then frowns and whispers, "Marina."

"Who?" I ask.

"Marina …" She repeats " … Shepard! Yeah, that was her. Marina Shepard!"

I grin. "Good stuff."

"Know I am."

I rise and head to the newspaper stand.

She stands and follows. "What'cha up to?"

"Just a hunch," I answer. "Her agency might be in the classifieds. Take a look. Might jog your memory."

She sighs wearily. "What the hell, I'm not doing anything."

We grab a paper each. I flick through mine and reach the classifieds. "Got her. She worked from home."

"What do you mean, worked?" Amber asks.

I tap the page opposite, indicating the death notices. "Predictaville 101. She's dead. Recently too."

"Car splatter?" Amber asks.

I look at her crossly. "The biggest entry's from an Oriana Shepard. Probably her mum. She could help."

"Yeah, good luck with that. How do we find her, genius?"

"Marina's address and number's right here." I tap the paper again. "Starting point."

Ambers shrugs. "Could work. She got a number?"

"Who doesn't?" I counter. "You got a phone?"

"Who doesn't?" she retorts.

"Me, dummy."

"Well shoot my butt off and call me an ar-"

"I get it." I hand her the paper with Marina's details. "Here."

She pulls out her phone, looks at the paper, types in the number, net-searches her name, and finds what we need. She's on the city outskirts.

I reach out to the main desk, grab a pen and scrap paper, write it down, then look out the window for the death car. "Our human mower's gone. I'm off. See ya."

I turn, making for the exit.

"Hey!" she calls, running after me. "You're gonna ditch me now?"

I stride out the door and down the steps.

She follows quickly. "You're so not splitting!"

I stop at the bottom and turn to her. "Oh, so I'm good enough for you, now?"

She comes to a halt. "What? Am I s'posed to lie down and wait for death-car to shoot back and flatten me?"

"Why not? You're good at being a *cross*-walk."

"Don't be such a bitch! That's my job!"

"You said it."

She frowns. "Crap." She shakes her head and sighs angrily. "As much as I hate your guts, small-boy, we go together. Got it?"

I shrug. "No choice."

"Good." She smacks my arm. "Jerk!"

Desk-girl sticks her head out the door. "Kiss her already!"

"Up yours!" we both yell at her.

She grins and goes back in.

Amber relents.

"You're right," she tells me. "We don't have a choice."

"About kissing?" I ask, confused.

She nearly explodes. "I'd tell you to kiss your own butt if your head wasn't so far up it."

"God, you drive me nuts …!"

"No, you're driving your own nuts. I'm outta here." She turns away.

"Yeah, you'll be safer at Marina's place!" I call.

She stops by a car, smacks the boot and turns back. "God! Where's your own damn car?"

"I walked here."

She fumes, points at the car and roars, "*Get in*!"

I head for it. "Hey, I saved you from being flattened …"

"I'd like to flatten you!" She pulls out her keys, presses a button and opens the door. "Get in before I snip your whipper! You're on thin ice, deadhead."

"And you're a crack up. Are we going? Or do you wanna stand here and bitch yourself off some more?"

She seethes, kicks a tyre and we both get in. Annoyed, she starts the car.

"Thanks," I say. "Only try not to drive me crazy."

She smacks the wheel, reverses hard and slams straight into another car.

A horn wails.

Defeated, she slumps onto the wheel, resting her head. "Now I know the universe is gunning for me. Oh shhhhh ..."

Rolling my eyes, I get out of the car.

Much later, we're in a lift, heading for the fourth floor of a rundown building. Amber's seething to hell from her broken fender, still swearing under her breath like she'd done the whole way here. The lift door opens with a *ding* and we step out, grimacing. The corridor's disgusting. Stinking. Freezing too, like the air conditioner's gone rogue.

We look down the corridor and see a door at the end with the number we need. We make for it, knowing it belonged to Marina Shepard.

We reach the door. A creak comes from behind it, indicating someone inside.

Hesitantly, I raise my hand and knock. The door's colder than the rest of the place.

Slow footsteps rise, the handle turns and the door squeaks open, revealing an old lady, hunched in the dim light.

Amber gasps.

The woman's ancient. Her skin's thinly stretched over her face, her hair whiter than snow. Her thin lips form into a line. A smirk. Like she knows us.

I speak cautiously. "Uh ... hi. I'm Sam. This is Amber."

Amber nods nervously. "Hey. Is this ... uh ... Marina Shepard's place?"

The old lady nods.

"Let me guess," I say, "Oriana Shepard?"

She nods again.

"You're related to Marina?" I press.

Silence.

I take a deep breath. "We'd like to learn a bit about her. Can we talk?"

She steps back slowly, raising a withered hand, indicating for us to enter.

Bracing ourselves, we head inside.

The fireplace is searing. The apartment, boiling. Beads of sweat trickle down my face. Amber's too. Weird, I think. So unlike the corridor outside.

We're seated before Oriana. A teacup, aromatically fragrant, sits by her side. Her face crumples into a mesh of wrinkles as she takes a sip, then stares at me hard, like I'm transparent. Her eyes lower to a section of floor nearby.

I look down. Part of it's glowing. Spinning. Like a Crystal Spinner.

I look up, meeting Oriana's gaze once more. "You see her, don't you?"

Oriana smiles mysteriously.

Amber's confused, not seeing Crystal at all.

"Psychoverse," she mutters. She glances from side to side. "Who's gonna spill?"

I pause, having no choice but to relent. "Okay ..." I begin, bracing for the backlash. "Your sister's ... not entirely ... dead."

Amber's eyes nearly pop out of her head. "So she's alive? A psycho's locked her up? What do you mean?"

I stay cautious. "Uh ... she's ... been with us all along. With me at least." She stares at me, horrified. "How? As a friggin' ghost?"

Oriana speaks. Her voice is crackly. Grating. Dried to the bone. "Spectretator."

Amber blinks, astounded. She shakes her head, her temper wins out and she shoots back with, "What the hell's that, a ghost potato?"

"A guide to the root of our troubles ..." Oriana cuts in.

Amber fumes, ready to blow. My jaw drops, horrified. She's probably just thinking of her sister but still ...

Thankfully, *very* thankfully, Amber keeps herself in check, drawing a sharp breath. "All I know's a busload of people's gone AWOL, a black car's gunned for my buns, hell-demons are in my family shots and my sister's hit the spirits! Where have we come to? Psychottica Coast?"

I indicate Oriana. "Yeah. Her *eye-land*. You can set sail anytime. Better be careful. It's rough out there."

Amber makes a face, then relents. "Fine. Whatever. So let's say I ..." She sighs wearily " ... go with this crap. You're saying a bus goes missing, taking my sister, and now she's back as a spirit guide? Why just her? Where's everyone else from the bus?" She stops, then gasps. "The freak in the pics Marina took. He went with the bus, didn't he?"

Silence.

"Yes," I conclude.

Oriana looks at her curiously. "While you ... didn't."

Amber's ready to blow again. "How do you know that you old ..."

I shoot her a death glance.

Amber sighs again, then swallows hard. "Not my fault I missed it. Had a bit too much fun the night before."

I speak softly. "That's why you're so cut up, isn't it?"

She nods glumly. "It was a feral pig of a way to go."

I bite my lip. "Sure was, but … you're right. Why's Crystal the odd one out?" I ponder this, then the truth hits home. "I get it. She wasn't sucked in by hell-demon."

Oriana's paper-like lips rise into a thin smile. She speaks croakily. "She was the youngest. The lightest. She fled, taking refuge in the village of …" Her voice lowers to a whisper " … Sanders Crossing."

Amber's taken aback. "Must be pretty deep in the hills."

"Deeper than you think," comes the reply.

Amber's ready to fire back.

I cut in quickly. "The others didn't make it there, did they?"

Oriana's voice darkens. "They were … gorged."

"Yeah, but there were no bodies," Amber points out.

"Unless," I counter, "They were sucked into *a* gorge? Like a chasm?"

Oriana nods. "Known to those who worship it as … the Pull-Pit."

Amber scoffs. "Oh yeah. Sweeping angels, burning hell realms …"

I slap her lightly.

She slaps me back " … and you're on Amber alert, hot stuff!"

Oriana continues. "The Pull-Pit's ashes fly high, thus marking his prey."

She glances at Amber's forehead, then mine. I touch my temple. It's as hot as hell.

Amber touches hers too. "What are you saying? That we've been dumped in hell-bad ash?"

Oriana speaks grimly. "His cinders burn many." She looks at me firmly. "Don't they?"

My heart drops like a lead balloon. "You mean we're targets?"

She speaks chillingly. "Your head aches. Your memories fly like the wind." Her voice croaks, drier than ever. "His silver blade blackens." Silence follows, then she draws a sharp breath. "Shadows darken my sight. I see no more." She stares into the flames. "Light is our saviour. Heat staves him off. For now. Yet, as the chosen, we too shall fall."

Amber huffs. "Speak for yourself. I don't get it. Who the hell are you talking about? Who's … shooting his fireballs at us?"

Oriana's head lowers in sorrow, her face overcome by shadows. "His names are many. His disciple calls him … the Galakir."

Amber scoffs again, looking away.

I focuson Oriana. "Can we stop him?"

71

She shuts her eyes. Her head rises, as if gazing afar. "The Pull-Pit devours life, thus widening its jaws. When all in reach is devoured, its jaws close." She bites her thin lip. "Be there only one way to seal it. Feeding on life opens the Pull-Pit. Thus it must …"

"… feed on death," I finish.

Amber's ready to go ape. "What are you saying? We throw a dead fish in there?"

"That'll only hook us in," I retort. "No, it's got to be big. Like …"

" … The Galakir himself," Oriana finishes. "That of the innocent opens the Pull-Pit. That of the guilty …"

"Closes it," I finish.

Amber's in disbelief. "How do you know so much, lady?"

Realisation strikes. "She's a survivor," I answer. "Like your sister. We're all linked to the big bad." The fire crackles grow, along with my insight. I give a small smile at Oriana. "You're from the Crossing, aren't you? Sanders Crossing. The place where Crystal went."

She speaks sadly. "I am."

Amber doesn't buy it. "Where is this damn place? Why can't we find it?"

"Same reason we can't find the Pull-Pit," I reply. "They're opposites. One light, one dark. They're links to …"

"Whatever," Amber cuts in, glaring at Oriana. "Where's the rest of your village? Wimping out?"

The old lady exhales wearily, opening her eyes. "Busy."

"Doing what?" she scoffs. "Playing cards while he plays snap?"

Oriana shifts slightly. "Let us say … there are greater threats to deal with. My kin were … are … needed."

"And you're not?" she huffs. She draws a sharp breath. "'Course not at your age."

I glare daggers at her.

She raises her hands. "'Kay. Sorry."

"Not as sorry as I am," Oriana replies.

I nod back at her. "You went up against him, didn't you? You got him into the Pull-Pit."

She sighs sadly. "You speak truly. We clashed, equal in strength. He was banished while I … paid dearly." She gazes high. "How old do you think I am?"

"Three hundred and fifty-" Amber begins.

I smack her again.

"Over eighty," I say.

"Wrong," she states. "I'm fifty-two years old."

Amber's jaw drops. "God lady, you must drink *a lot* of bourbon. *Now* it makes sense."

Oriana sneers. "Your cockiness will be the death of you, girl. As you would say, cockiness leads to a cock-up."

Amber raises a finger. "Okay, you're getting good. So why's he back from the dead?"

I frown in thought. Logic dawns. "His disciple."

Oriana scowls. "A woman. Young. Naive. Deceived." She almost spits at the memory. "She returned to the Pull-Pit, casting the blood of the innocent into …"

"Bloody hell," Amber finishes, running a hand over her face.

"Exactly," Oriana confirms. "All while I was confined to this …" She indicates the room bitterly "… prison. My kin could do little but watch from … afar."

My mind's on the disciple.

"A woman?" I ponder.

"Car-bitch!" Amber realises. She purses her lips, annoyed. "Why's she doing his dirty work? He's a hell-demon, he can blow us all away. If my sis can show herself, why can't he?"

"'Cause he'll stand out like a severed thumb in daylight," I say. "Your sis is also lighter and brighter than he is. She can get away with it."

"Leaving us on his menu," Amber states. "Talk about a hell-appetite." She scowls. "Why us? I know I'm hot stuff but still …"

My gaze rises to the mantle over the fireplace. A framed photo's there, showing a young woman holding a baby. The woman's clearly Oriana. The child …

"Marina," I whisper. "Marina Shepard." I lean forward, elbows on my knees and hands clasped as I say to Oriana. "Your daughter." I pause. "She's not dead, is she?"

Oriana sniffs, looking away.

I continue. "When our hell-demon knew you were on the warpath, he made her his disciple as the ultimate payback. She won't come for you. Not her mother, but …"

" … We're food for thought," Amber cuts in. "What I don't get is why she took shots of me and my sis? What's the point?"

"Hunters scout their prey," I reply. "He was sniffing you out."

"Sounds disgusting," Amber retorts.

I move to nudge her.

She smacks my arm away. "But he can't see Ghost-Chrissy now?"

"She'd be sucked into hell if he could," I answer.

"True," says Oriana. "Her influence so far, has been … fleeting. She's only spoken to you, boy, through the mouths of other's, else the hunter's scent would have been … sparked."

"So where to from here?" I focus on the photo. "Finding Marina's out of the picture. She won't say anything. Sounds like no one's at the Crossing either. The only way to fix this is by …"

" … going in for the kill," Amber and I chorus.

We lock gazes, glad we're on the same wavelength.

"We'll be targets," I say grimly.

"Got no choice," Amber says back. "Kill or be killed, man."

I look at Oriana firmly. "We're going to the Pull-Pit to finish what you started."

Amber grimaces at Oriana's wrinkled face. "As long as we don't end up looking like … that."

I elbow her.

"Sorry," she adds.

"Not as sorry as I'll be if we don't get the Galakir into the Pull-Pit," I reply.

"The price is high," Oriana states. She glances at the glowing floor. "Yet there's always a little light on things. A spark of hope, shall we say."

Amber's eyes widen. "Chrissy? You mean–"

She stops dead, hit by an icy wind.

The fireplace's flames flicker, touched by the chill.

Oriana's face drops.

"What the hell's that?" Amber asks shakily.

I look at the floor. Crystal's glow's retreating to the front door. Slowly, she slides under it, vanishing from sight.

"He's here," I whisper. My mind races. "Why now?"

"Attraction," Oriana answers.

Amber looks around nervously. "There's better ways of hitting on a girl."

74

"Yeah, and he'll hit hard," I warn. "He's got a grudge against your sister and Oriana here, and we've brought him right in." I rise from my seat with Amber following. I reach for Oriana when …

Creaaaaaaak!

The bedroom floorboards.

From behind the closed door.

They're being walked on.

A drawn-out groan rises.

Squelch!

Blood appears at the top of the door, trickling down and drenching the wood in thick black ooze. More trails out from under it, wavering over the wooden floor like outstretched fingers.

Amber retreats, horrified. "Unholy sh—"

The flames dim further.

Oriana rises.

"Outside!" she snaps, pushing us away, albeit weakly. "Take refuge in the city streets where many walk."

Amber shoots for the front door. She pulls the handle.

Locked.

Squeak!

The bedroom door slowly opens. A long shadow stretches out, touching the fireplace's dying flames, killing them.

Amber clutches me tightly.

I grab her instinctively. Protectively, like she's the most important thing in the world.

Smash!

The window bursts open in tingling shards as Crystal's golden glow soars in, sweeping into the bedroom. Savage roars ignite. Blinding flashes follow in a fierce fusion of fire and ice as a chilling wind gust hits us hard.

We struggle to stay upright.

Click!

The front door opens, swinging in.

I bolt into the corridor, wrenching Amber along.

A thunderous roar hurtles Crystal from the bedroom. She flails wildly, spinning back through the smashed window, plummeting away.

Oriana staggers for the front door.

Slam!

The door thunders shut, sealing her inside, then locks with a click.

I grab the handle and pull.

Sealed tight.

I thump it hard.

"Don't be a tosser!" Amber yells, pulling me down the hallway.

We stumble away, past the lift, reach the staircase, then …

"*Yaaaaaaaargh …!*"

Oriana's hysterical screams explode from behind the door. A blood-curdling squelch erupts, silencing her.

I boot the stairway door open and we shoot through.

We run into the street, merging with the crowd. They're ready to party, blind to anything but themselves.

Screech!

A car veers onto the pavement, speeding right at us. I grab Amber and we dive aside, crashing into a trash can, toppling it loudly. The car veers away, roaring off, with several kids raising their phones and taking shots.

Amber swallows hard. "Car-Bitch!"

I help her up, thinking ahead. "Pull-Pit."

We hurry past the kids who only care about posting crap on their phones.

"Do you even know where to find the damn thing?" Amber calls.

A swirling glow comes from a street sign, growing steadily brighter.

Crystal.

"I've got a fair idea," I reply.

Amber follows my gaze, then stops dead. "Whoa!"

I hold her hand. "You see her now?"

She's too starstruck to notice. "Sis?"

The golden cloud swirls in the neon light. Nobody notices, thank god. Their phones ensure that. We watch as Crystal tenses, now with a slight red streak. A cut from the Galakir, I reason. She tenses further, summoning her strength, then streaks off into the night like a shooting star.

Amber swallows hard, sniffs, wipes a tear from her eye, then notices her hand in mine. She pulls it away roughly. "What do you think you're doing? I'm not up for grabs."

"I'm not buying," I say, striding off. "Come on. We're needed."

She runs after me. "And you're going in unloaded? We need to stock up first."

"With what?

"Got stuff at home. Might help."

I stop, turning to her. "Oh yeah. You're gonna fight Satan with a baseball bat?"

She shrugs. "Used it on an ex and he was just as bad. There's more too. Ropes and things."

"Seriously?"

"Got a survival course coming up."

"Why am I not surprised?" I look around. "Fine. We'll hit your house but we better be quick. We're not safe on our own. Hope you're stuff's ready."

"Totally. Kit's ready to go. Maybe more." She smiles sneakily.

"I believe you." I inhale sharply as we make for her car. "Maybe just a little too much."

The city lights fade as Amber drives us into the hills. A rucksack's in the back. She'd dashed in and out of her house, her gear ready. I want to ask what's in the bag but know I'd dread the answer. An Olympic-like fire torch, care of her street-performing brother, sits over the bag, lighter by its side. Good move, I tell her. Heat staves him off. She says she'd love us to be in a hot nightclub full of people. That won't protect us from Marina, I point out. We can't run or hide. We'll be dead if we do. No, I vow. This ends tonight.

We reach the road where the bus vanished. Amber's phone beeps and dies, fading like our spirits. I tell her not to be surprised since this whole place is draining. She tosses the phone back at me, swearing grumpily and driving on.

The moonbeams rise, along with Crystal's golden glow. We follow in awe, guided by her swirling tendrils. Talk about lifting our spirits, I quip. Amber smirks and tells me to shut up.

The moonbeams soon vanish, overtaken by the clawing finger-like branches of the rotting trees. Crystal leads us off the main road, then disappears down a narrow path too thin to drive down.

Amber switches the engine off. "Hellsville 101."

We step out of the car. The air's icy.

I look around grimly. "Pull-Pit's close."

Amber agrees. "Suck central."

We open the back doors. Amber grabs the knapsack. I grab the torch, stuffing the lighter into my pocket.

"You're not gonna light that sucker?" Amber asks, astounded. "Aren't we s'posed to melt the crap out of him?"

"Heat stands out, dummy," I reply, "and this place is freezing. The torch won't burn for long. Wind doesn't help either."

"Not with your gasbagging."

Crystal's glow rises ahead.

"Way to go sis," Amber murmurs.

I head in slowly, with her following. Crystal inches back, cautiously guiding us along the gravel pathway. The wind grows colder. The ground, slippery. Many dead trees, half-fallen, lean on each other for support. Mangled branches form a long archway ahead.

Amber shivers. "Whose stupid idea was this?"

"Ours," I reply.

"Bite me," she shoots back.

Hissssss …!

She yelps, recoiling into my arms.

More hisses follow.

"Sh-" Amber begins.

"Shut it," I warn, clasping a hand on her mouth.

She smacks it away and looks into the trees. They're filled with snakes. Every kind. Pythons to worms, they're all there, tongues flickering hungrily.

Crystal enters, prompting us to follow.

Amber shudders. "No way in hell."

I clasp her hand. "Thought you were strong stuff."

"Only on you."

"Bully."

"Moron."

I clasp it tighter. "Now you're getting it. Show 'em, huh?"

She pulls her hand away, swearing under her breath.

Step by slow step, I guide her along, following Crystal.

The snakes watch slyly.

She quivers.

"Easy," I tell her. "Almost there."

We reach the end of the archway. No snakes are beyond it. We run out, stumbling down a slope and then …

Whoosh!

A fierce wind hits us hard.

Amber yelps, falling forward. "Whoa!"

I grab her arm, pulling her back from the gaping black chasm. We regain our balance, shivering in the exhaling currents from its mighty jaws.

A frosty wind gust brushes my face. My mind tingles, feeling an affinity with it. I blink hard.

Oriana's words return. *'Your head aches. Your memories fly like the wind. His silver blade blackens.'*

What I said follows. *'We're all linked to the big bad.'*

Amber gazes at the chasm. "The damn Pull-Pit." She sees my face. "What, do you want to be converted? Move!"

Her words hit home.

We retreat. My mind lightens, slightly, then …"

Flash!

Crystal.

By the side of the Pull-Pit. Glowing, transparent, and in human form.

Amber's jaw drops, stunned by the sight of her ghostly sister.

"Chrissy," she whispers. "Oh my god …"

Crystal smiles, then winces, pointing behind us with a silent scream.

We whirl around.

A tall figure looms in the shadows.

Amber cringes. "That's the bastard?"

A bellowing snarl erupts, shaking the trees.

We recoil, almost blown away.

"Son of a-" Amber growls, reaching into her pocket and pulling out a dart.

"What the hell's that gonna do?" I cry.

"Make me feel a lot better," she retorts.

Swish!

She hurls it straight into the shadows for a direct hit.

I blink, surprised by her throw. "Impressive."

"Yep," Amber nods. "Got the mother f-…"

"Duck!" Crystal wails.

We drop as the dart flies back at us, shooting over our heads and falling by the chasm's edge.

Slowly, heavily, the Galakir staggers from the shadows, one leg dragging behind the other, scraping over the dirt. Like in the photo, his head's lopped sideways, glaring grotesquely. Unlike Crystal, he's solid. Real to the bloodied bone. His head straightens a little, staring right at me.

I gasp.

Like I'm looking into a mirror.

He snarls. A long, forked tongue hisses from his black lips, fangs on either side.

Amber's unfazed.

"Pffft!" she scoffs. "I've taken out cheating bastards for more."

Her voice snaps me back to reality. I pull the lighter from my pocket, hold it by the torch and click it, setting the torch alight.

He snarls, letting loose with a sharp breath. An icy wind gust sweeps over the flames. They don't go out. Looking aside, I see Crystal, brow furrowed, keeping the flame alive.

He staggers in.

"This is bulldust!" Amber snaps. She reaches into her knapsack, pulling out a gun.

"Where the hell'd you get that?" I cry.

She drops the knapsack. "What, you think I'm gonna go on a survival course unprepped? Darts and flaming torches, my butt. What is this? The Middle Ages?" She aims the gun at him, growling, "Suck this into your Pull-Pit!"

Bang!

She blows a hole in his chest.

He stops briefly, then staggers on again, still dragging one foot behind the other.

She lets rip with another shot, shooting him in the head. Streams of black blood pour down his face. A third blast gets his shoulder. The next gets his neck. She fires again and again, hitting him square on.

Click!

She's out.

He lunges with a roar, smacking the gun from her hand. She recoils as I charge in, swiping the torch. He smacks it away, then lashes out with a fierce backhand, striking me hard. I flail sideways as he grabs Amber's throat, pulls her in and opens his mouth wide. She gurgles loudly as his long snake-like tongue surges in.

I grab the flaming torch and push myself up, ramming its searing tip into his side. His tongue retracts as his freezing body drowns the flames, before his chilling arm sweeps down, grabbing my neck too, and pulling me up. He stares straight at me, peering into my eyes.

With recognition.

He grins grotesquely, then speaks in a deathly low monotone.

"*Sooooon ...*"

Amber chokes hard. Her hand flails, reaching desperately into her pocket and pulling out another dart. She growls furiously, then slams the metal tip into his eye, loosening his grip. She and I struggle out, falling back, hitting the ground and rolling away. She reaches her knapsack, fumbles desperately and pulls out a hunting knife.

"How much crap have you got in there?" I cry.

She aims and hurls fiercely.

Squelch!

The blade rams through his other eye, next to the dart.

Amber grabs the dead torch, leaps up and lunges, smashing his head sideways and releasing a trickle of blood that lands on her knapsack. He roars, recoiling to the Pull-Pit's edge. She lashes the torch viciously, ramming him in the face and sending the hunting knife squelching out the back of his skull. Enraged, she swings again, belting him hard. He shoots back, flailing into the engulfing darkness with a bellowing roar before fading from sight.

She scowls triumphantly, clasping the torch. "Now that's what you call a bat *into* hell!"

I sigh wearily. "Yeah, and you always make an impact. Just not enough to get a head off the rest." I draw a sharp breath and glance down.

She follows my gaze. "Oh, crap ..."

His black blood's fizzled into the knapsack, leaving only a stain. Nothing big enough to rub into the dirt.

The ground rumbles. Tremors grow. Harder. Louder. Shockwaves ripple, uprooting a hollow tree and sending it spiralling into the Pull-Pit.

Crystal wails, pointing back the way we came. We turn to the snake archway, its shaking dead trees ready to implode. I grab Amber's hand and we bolt for it, struggling to keep our balance. Her swearing grows with the rising quakes as we enter the archway, zigzagging through it.

Plop!

She yelps as a snake drops past us, then another, then another. She smacks them away with the torch and we run on.

A taipan makes for her leg. She screams.

Whoosh!

A chilling wind gust surges in, hoisting the snake up and pulling it back. We feel the pull too, but not as bad. We glance back, seeing the snake sucked into the Pull-Pit by a furious vacuum. More snakes follow, rising by the dozen. We duck as their slimy, slithering bodies flail over us in waves, sweeping into the chasm and falling in a hideous hissing mass.

Finally, they're no more.

The wind picks up. My arm jerks back with it as if pulled by a magnet. My leg goes too, skidding along the dirt.

Now the Pull-Pit's got us.

"Damn thing's worked up an appetite," I murmur.

Amber cringes grimly. "So what are we? Dessert?"

"Pretty much," I answer. "God knows why. You're not that sweet."

"You're the sourpuss!" she snaps. The pull grows. "Why do I always get sucked into this crap?"

Creak!

A rotting tree uproots, flying past us into the Pull-Pit. The suction grows. We grit our teeth, skidding back for the chasm.

A glow sweeps in.

Crystal.

She shoots by, engulfing us in her spirit. Energised by her golden touch, we break free from the Pull-Pit's hold and run through the archway. Crystal releases us, flying ahead for the main road. Amber's relieved to see it's closer than we thought. Crystal flies up a slope then stops, spinning over the highway.

"Light at the end of the tunnel," I whisper.

We run on, reach the end, stagger up the slope onto the main road, then turn back, looking at the fallen archway.

"Crap almighty," Amber whispers.

I peer into the shadows. A woman's followed us out. She's heading sideways, hidden by the shadows, making for a car in the distance.

"Marina," I whisper.

The Pull-Pit roars, breaking my focus. Crystal retreats, along with Amber.

Bang!

A black blast shoots high, engulfing the bushland in a shadowy dome. Crystal clutches us tightly. We cover our eyes amid the carnage of the dying bushland while trying to block out the wind's screeching howl. The rumbles reach breaking point, before the dome blows out in a deafening bellow.

Amber falls on me, I lose my balance, and we hit the road in a heap. The sick blast shoots over us, soars into the night, then dissipates. Turning our heads sideways, we see that the archway, the snakes, and the Pull-Pit are gone, leaving only devastated bushland.

Silence follows.

Amber breaks it, sarcastically. "Not good, huh?"

Another roar erupts.

An engine this time.

We yelp and roll sideways, tumbling down the slope, rolling into a tree and seeing Marina's car shoot by. We watch as it skids down the road, races 'round the bend and vanishes from sight.

"Car bitch!" Amber seethes. She shrugs. "What the hell? This day can't get any worse. Might as well go for it."

"Go for wh– mmmf."

She plants her lips on mine and kisses. Hard. Strangely, I don't fight back, embracing her wholeheartedly. Finally, we part, smiling.

"Now that's what I call the kiss of life," I say.

"More like the kiss of death," she replies, "but I love it."

I grin. "You know what? Me too."

We kiss again, longer this time, then part once more.

I smile. "We seem to have a knack for going up against gaping chasms."

She indicates where the Pull-Pit's been. "While I get stuck with the two biggest buttholes on earth."

We smirk and come together again.

An engine rises in the distance. An ordinary car this time. I wonder why Marina hasn't returned for us, then find myself not caring.

I've enough to distract me for now.

Amber's car's clunky, thanks to the bushland blowout. We only just make it to a roadhouse before the car conks out.

The place is still open. Even better, they give us a room for the night. No one says anything about the bushland chaos, and we don't ask. We'll hear about it soon enough. Marina's bound to head back there too. Right now, we don't care. We go to our room, crash heavily, and sleep like logs.

I awake first, finding it well into the next day. I rise from the bed, go out to the balcony and look at the bush, absorbing its natural aroma. Despite its peace, I'm still on edge. This isn't over. The Galakir's blood never hit the sand, so it's not a matter of *if* he comes back, but when. Marina'll make sure of that. What gets me most is what Oriana had said.

'Your head aches. Your memories fly like the wind. His silver blade blackens ...'

My thoughts race.

"Morning, butthead," Amber says, walking sleepily onto the balcony.

"Morning, hell witch," I say back.

She sits beside me, puts her arm in mine, and rests her head on my shoulders. "We rock, huh?"

"Yeah," I reply. "We did good."

We kiss lightly, our hearts aglow. We part, smiling at each other, then she turns to the bushland. I go to wrap my arm 'round her, then stop dead, staring at her forehead. A black mark's streaked from temple to temple. Transparent, jagged, and throbbing wildly.

Oriana's words return. *'His cinders burn many.'*

My forehead throbs too.

I tense, watching her mark pulsate, then vanish. She hasn't felt anything, nor has she seen mine. That's obvious. I swallow hard, knowing the worst.

We're still marked.

"Why now?" I whisper, gazing at Amber's forehead. "Why didn't I see it before?"

She snuggles into my shoulder. "Because you love me and you're dumb." She looks at the sky, then sits up rapidly. "Oh my friggin' god!"

I follow her gaze, seeing a swirling mist. Not a cloud but ...

"Chrissy," Amber whispers.

I hug her tightly, knowing why I saw the beast's mark on her. She'd been ... high-lighted.

Amber's in awe. She clutches my hand warmly.

"Thanks," she whispers. "For everything."

"You're welcome," I reply.

"Not you," she retorts, slapping me lightly. She relents. "Well, yeah, you too. A bit."

"A bit?" I say back. "God, you're always looking for a piece of me, aren't you?"

"Yeah, and it's not the piece you're thinking of." She looks past Crystal, seeing the rising black clouds approaching. "Storm's coming. God, you're cursed."

My forehead prickles, sharper than ever.

84

"More so than you think," I reply.

She sighs, thinking I meant her. "You're a knob." She kisses my cheek.

I don't move.

She looks at me. "What?"

"Just thinking," I answer.

"What else is new?" she scoffs. "'Bout what?"

"Marina, the Galakir …"

"Geeze, lighten up," she retorts, then indicates her sister. "We're … god forbid, a family now." She stops, horrified at what she's said, and almost spits, disgusted. "God damn!"

Crystal shimmers brightly.

"You're right," I say, hugging her. "We're a family …" My voice lowers "For *now* …" We stare at the sky, seeing the distant lightning streaks " … But a storm's coming and when it does …" My voice lowers to a whisper "All hell'll break loose."

Meridian's speaker crackles with static, rising with the chilling breeze over the bloodied body.

I stare at the pages. Dangling threads hang like a noose around my neck, linking me into a chain of events. I'm starting to see those links. They're hooking me into every sick tale, leaving me hanging, but it's too soon to jump to conclusions. I need clear-cut answers. God, I hate that term.

I pick up the next story and grimace.

Terminal Madness.

Fitting.

Very fitting.

Chapter Five

Terminal Madness

The rage is boiling over.

I struggle desperately through the rising mob, battling the hardcore mania.

I came to the City to sort out a bill. All I'd wanted was to cross the street to reach an office. A protest rally hit first, streaming out of nowhere, sweeping me up and blocking every way out.

I'm pushed against a man.

"Can you—" I begin.

He thrusts me into a big guy. Big guy shoves me back. I hit a woman, before being whirled around to bounce off a teenager. I swear furiously. What the hell am I? A tennis ball to be bounced around by a bunch of tossers?

I cry out. No one hears me in this hate tsunami. The chants grow louder, then …

Thump!

I smack into a solid guy behind me. Two strong hands grab my shoulders, pulling me through the streaming mass, thrusting me to the edge of the crowd. We erupt out of it, hitting the side of the street. Whoever's clutching me doesn't let go. Their grip tightens as I'm pushed along, picking up speed as we stumble over the footpath to the edge of an alleyway. Despite the surging rally, the alleyway's empty. Shadowy too, with a musty stench. We splash through the murky puddles as I'm shoved hard.

"Hey!" I snap. "You can't– mmmmf!"

A gloved hand clamps over my mouth. The guy's strong. I struggle furiously. We turn into a backstreet where I'm released and thrown ahead. The world blurs as I hit the ground, falling into a slimy puddle near a closed garage door. I fully expect a kick to follow but ...

Nothing.

I look up at the guy.

"What the hell ...?"

They're draped in black robes. A hood covers their face. A belt wraps their sturdy waist, showing a grotesque skull. Going by the weirdos in the rally, he wouldn't have stood out.

He reaches into his robes, pulling out a dagger.

I leap up to run.

Another freak, dressed the same, steps out from the corner, blocking my path. I stop dead. This one's carrying a sword.

Terrified, I inch back, retreating for the garage door.

Squeeeeeeak!

The metal door rises. I back off, hitting the side wall as the door slides up, slowly reaching its peak. A figure steps out. He's not like the others. No robes, just a business suit. He's tall, with olive skin and slicked black hair. His eyes are narrow, his nose pointed and his jaw hard. He sneers cruelly, like he knows me.

He steps in, speaking in a thick Spanish accent. "Bet you weren't s'pecting to see me so soon, uh?"

His voice is familiar. I frown. I've never met him before but sense a connection. "What-?"

Thud!

His solid kick hurls me against the dumpster. I drop to the ground, gasping. Another sharp kick knocks the wind out of me. He steps in and puts his foot on my head, pressing half my face into a slimy puddle. The foul, murky water half-covers my nose and mouth as I struggle back. His foot keeps me in place. The tip of his shoe presses into my ear, making me wince.

Flick!

A switchblade.

He leans down, bringing the knife close to my face. "Let's *cut* the talk, compadre!"

The blade touches my cheek. I cringe as it's pressed in, barely hearing a rising engine roar, before ...

Screech!

A black van veers 'round the corner, skids, brakes, and hits the robed freaks with a sickening thud. They slam against the alley wall, slumping in a heap. How the van got here so fast is beyond me. The protest rally was too big for *anything* to shoot through. I watch, astounded, as the freaks who've just been body-slammed into a brick wall, rise smoothly, untouched.

The van's doors slide open. Two men leap out, splashing into the alleyway, holding crossbows, not loaded with arrows, but darts.

Thuk!

Thuk!

The darts flash into the freak's hoods, sending them slumping back down. This time, they don't rise.

I sit up, rubbing my face, as Spanish-guy retreats into the garage. His fist strikes out, hitting a button on the wall, then sneers as the door drops with surprising speed, slamming shut.

The world blurs, making me wince.

The men move in. One kneels, flashing a torch in my eye. I blink and look away. The other whips out a device, scans me, then looks at the readings.

"It's him," he confirms.

A woman calls from the driver's seat. "We gotta go!"

They grab my arms. Shards of pain ripple through me as I'm picked up, carried to the van, hoisted into the back and dropped onto its metal floor. Nausea overtakes me, along with enveloping darkness. With my last ounce of strength, I mutter, "I should so pay my bills online …"

Then everything goes black.

***

Splinters of light pierce my vision.

My eyes open groggily. I give an agonised groan. I'm on a bed. Sterile air wafts through my nostrils. Memory fragments return, albeit slowly. The damn crowd. The superhuman assassins. Spanish–guy …

"He's back."

The voice is female.

The van driver.

I blink hard. The lights are dim. The place, humming. Footsteps rise over a grilled floor. The whole place is metal. Like a prison.

Four hazy faces swirl in my vision, coming into focus. The woman, in her mid-fifties, sits on a chair by my bed. A white-haired man's beside her, also on a chair. Two more men, one hard-faced, the other not so much, stand behind them. I recognise them from the van. Like her, they're also a lot older than me. All four wear metal cuffs, flickering with tiny lights, on their right wrists.

I struggle to sit up, groan, then slump back down.

"Easy," the old man says.

"Somebody wanna tell me …" I murmur, " … what the story is."

Silence.

I find the strength to sit up. It hurts like hell. I cough. The woman gives me a glass of water. I drink it, relishing its refreshing taste.

"Better talk fast," I say wearily. "I want to go home."

She puts the empty glass on a table.

The hard-faced man speaks sharply. "You're not going anywhere."

"You can go to hell," I shoot back.

The woman cuts in, asking, "Do you remember your name?"

Her gaze is warm. Loving. Unnerving.

"Sam," I reply uneasily. Sam Silver."

She bites her lip sadly, looking away. The old man frowns, Hard-face scowls and the other man sighs.

A stab of pain hits my side. I wince loudly.

The woman leans in quickly.

"Easy," she says gently. "You were pretty beat up."

I nod, recalling the alleyway. One word sticks out. A name.

I glance at each of them. "Wanna tell me what's going on?"

Clang!

Squeak!

A rat's scurrying through a vent.

"Got no choice," Hard-face seethes.

The old man nods. "No." He sits forward, interlocking his fingers. "We'll have to start over."

"So what?" I conclude. "We've met before?"

The woman speaks shakily. "You were … special. To all of us." She swallows hard. "Me more than anyone …" She pauses " … Adam."

I frown, taking this in. "What are you? My mother? I'm adopted, is that what you're saying?"

Her face falls.

Hard-face snickers.

The older man speaks. "What year were you born?"

"You know everything, you tell me," I retort.

"Please," he presses. "It's important."

Sighing, I tell him.

He nods again. "Makes sense." He pauses. "You're Sam Silver ... now. Long ago, however, you were ..." He inhales sharply "... Adam Spears."

I shake my head, confused. "What's that mean? I was mind-wiped?"

"In a sense," he answers. His head rises, announcing, "Adam Spears died two years before you were born."

I struggle to take this in. "You guys are nuts ..."

Hard-Face scowls. "You want us to take you up top and throw you back on the street?"

"So get the cops!" I snap.

"And say what?" he snaps back. "They won't help you. Just the opposite."

"While you're doing a great job!" I retort. "What is this place? Jail?"

"Your vision," the older man reveals.

I look at him, aghast. "Seriously?"

"Seriously," he relents.

The woman looks at him too. "There's no choice, Hawkron."

He sighs. "No. There's not."

She looks back at me, speaking hesitantly. "Decades ago, I met Cutter there ..." She glances at Hard-face, before indicating the other man, " ... and Spark ... at uni. Then we met you ... Adam." She sniffs, haunted by the memory.

Spark speaks. "We hung out a lot. Sure, you could drink anyone under the table, but you had brains too. You were an idealist. Better than anybody."

"Such a comedown," Cutter scoffs bitterly.

The older man takes up the story. " 'Til a drunk driver hit you crossing the street. You survived, naturally, but were never the same again. What you had, is what's called an NDE. A ..."

"I know," I cut in. "A near death experience."

"Yes," he confirms. "Whatever you ... saw ... overtook you, consuming every waking moment. You spoke of a revelation. That you knew the very nature of life itself. You believed in the music of the stars, and that we're all comprised of universal frequencies, solidified into individuals filled with sole-

our energy. You believed that no one can ever be killed, and that in the end, we'll all be healed, to be absorbed back into the universe as a whole." He indicates the woman. "You convinced Mojo first, then Cutter and Spark."

"So where do you come in ...?" I ask, prompting his name.

"Hawkron," he responds, smiling gently. "I was your lecturer."

I blink, astounded.

He continues. "I must admit that even I was ... blown away, as you put it. Your passion grew, converting others to our cause and reaching the highest levels of private ventures, resulting in ..." He glances at the roof " ... this."

"Now *that* was a miracle," Spark says. "Financial backing's not cheap for a research station, 'specially one taking a stab in the dark."

"Literally," Mojo adds.

"Pffft," I scoff. "What's it all for?"

Hawkron speaks cautiously. "You believed that if, at the point of death, we placed a Tracer on a subject's energy field, we could track their frequency to see where they'd end up after passing over. Your theory was to grab them and reverse their death, no matter how long they'd been gone for, thereby healing them."

I frown, taking this in.

Hawkron goes on. "Your first ... *our* first act ... was to select subjects with a terminal disease ..."

"To kill them?" I clarify.

"No," Mojo corrects firmly. "They agreed to it. Your talked so ... passionately ... that they ended up *wanting* to die. They weren't going to live long anyway and–"

"We killed them!" I counter bitterly.

Cutter sneers. "How the mighty have fallen."

"That's life!" I snap.

"That's death!" Cutter shoots back.

"That's neither," Hawkron cuts in. "Life and death are like gases, changing from solids to fluids and back again. We've all been through it countless times, only that car smack sent you in consciously."

"Well it's sure worn off now," I retort.

Mojo looks at the others, speaking grimly. "We've got to show him. There's no choice."

Cutter's face falls.

"She's right," Spark says. "We can't win him over."

Cutter sneers, looking away.

"Show me what?" I ask.

Mojo stands and heads to a wheelchair by the door, bringing it in. "There's no point talking, Adam. Time's running out. For all of us." She helps me into it.

My side ripples in agony.

"God," I cringe. "I feel like death warmed up."

"Just the opposite," Spark corrects. "You're life cooled down."

"Says the bright Spark," I retort.

Mojo smiles. "Haven't changed, have you Adam? We're grateful for that."

"I wish I was," I mutter. "Wherever we're going better be worth it." I sigh wearily. "Talk about dying to see it."

Mojo pushes my wheelchair along the narrow, metal passageway. The wheels squeak loudly over the grilled floor and mechanised humming.

I look around curiously. "Where are we? Still in the city?"

"Below it," Spark answers. "*Way* below."

"Our base is nearly as big," Mojo explains. "That's how we saved you up top. We couldn't have got through the protest rally otherwise. We made it just in time."

"Saving you from those bloody Corpmuscles," Cutter scowls.

"Who?" I ask.

"Big bad's lifeblood," comes the bitter reply.

"Flowing from the heart of the problem," I conclude. "What's with their hoods and swords? What are they? Recycled crap from the Middle Ages?"

"Static crap," Cutter corrects.

Hawkron nods. "They don't believe in the young, or the old, just an eternal middle age. They're an ancient order, relying on blades and armour."

"Are we safe in here?"

"For now," Mojo answers. "The base's energies keep us hidden. Cutter here wanted to call it the Regurgitator. We vetoed that."

I note their wristbands. "What are they? Com-Links?"

"Far more," Hawkron answers. "True, we use them to keep in contact, but they also bypass the base's security systems. Their grip's tight, but we have to put up with that until I can fix them, which isn't easy with this alloy."

"Doesn't matter," Cutter scowls. "Their pain gives us the edge."

"While you run amok," I retort. "What does that make 'em? Terror-Wrists?"

Mojo smirks. "No, but that's a good name."

We reach the corridor's end. Cutter puts his band on the door pad.

Hiss!

The door slides up. We head in, entering an Operations room. A terminal stands in its centre, overlooked by a wallscreen, split into several digital screens.

Cutter smacks a switch. The biggest screen changes to a world map filled with shifting, wavering, multi-coloured patterns. "Here's your vision … boss!" The last word spits scornfully off his tongue.

Hawkron approaches the terminal and flicks another switch, highlighting several clouds.

"Let me guess," I say. "You're tracking the dead."

"Correct," Hawkron replies. "The lightest shoot to the heavens. The heaviest fall back into the dirt to regrow."

"Yeah," Cutter scowls. "Welcome back, *kid*."

Hawkron points to part of the screen. "See, that green patch near the Andes? That's where the lightest frequencies flock. Heaven knows why. We believe a super-natural element there attracts them."

I shake my head. "This whole place's dodgy. I'm not surprised things went belly-up."

"No, just you for a while," Cutter retorts.

"Indeed," Hawkron agrees. "You'd just started your plans for the base when a …" He pauses " … terminally-ill test subject offered to help us out. There was no time to argue. They were insistent."

I frown, sensing his tone. "Things went wrong, didn't they?"

Mojo sniffs sadly, taking up the story. "Our tech wasn't ready. When you … uh … saw how bad our subject was, you made the choice to …" She whimpers, choking up.

"… be their lifeline," Hawkron finishes. "To guide them back to their body."

"But you lost us both?" I conclude.

Mojo nods. "There was a Tracer glitch. Not only that, you'd had a great life and your resonance shot for the stars. You tried taking our test subject, but their life had been much harder, leaving 'em solidified to the core. You went up and they went down, dropping into a hell of a place." She pauses.

"It took a decade for them to surface. Even more for you to come down to earth. You hit the ground running, moving too fast for us to trace, so a few friends …" She nods at the colours on the screen " … went in to find you."

I shiver. "I never thought anyone'd be dying to see me."

"*They* certainly did," she confirms, "and succeeded … eventually. That's how we got to you up top."

She rubs my shoulder warmly.

I shift awkwardly, pulling away. "What about our test subject? The one I went in after? What happened to them?"

All four go silent, like a heavy cloud's dropped.

"What?" I ask, warily.

Cutter speaks bitterly. "Things went wrong for 'em. Too *bloody* wrong. Thanks to you, genius, they got a huge smackdown, leaving 'em with a split psyche." His face hardens. "Now they're *really* lost. Life doesn't want 'em, death doesn't either. Their mind's screwed, their body's twisted, and they want payback for what you did to 'em, leaving us in hell's firing line."

Hawkron takes up the story. "Most people forget about their past lives. This … freak of nature … recalls the lot. They couldn't get into the base, so hacked its system, using our tech to locate death's heavier residue. Before we knew it, they'd found, solidified and assimilated their fellow anomalies … into disciples."

"Why?" I ask, astounded. "So we can keep coming back from the dead, killing each other over and over?"

"They want what we have," Hawkron states.

"What you started!" Cutter snaps.

"This place," Mojo says softly. "To grow their order."

Cutter sneers. "Leaving us with a war on our hands. Thanks for that."

"Hey, you helped set it up," I retort.

"I lost my whole damn family because of you!" he roars back.

"Well bringing 'em back shouldn't be a problem!".

"Enough!" Mojo cries, raising her hands. "Please! Let it go."

"Thanks to him we can't let *anything* go!" Cutter growls. He kicks the wall loudly.

Mojo jumps.

The station creaks again.

I pause, letting things ease. "We got a name for death's reject?"

Hawkron looks at the screen. "Like you, they've changed too much from who they once were. Now they're back from the dead we call them, the Ex-Terminated."

I shrug. "Like the name."

Spark shrugs back. "Us too."

"Was he the guy up top?" I ask, thinking of Spanish-guy.

Cutter shakes his head. "No. He's the Ex-Terminated's head honcho, Varkos. The wimp bolted but we got those Corpmuscles. They're locked in the Incubators."

"The what?" I press.

"Holding cells," Hawkron answers. "Killing them means losing them, and they'll only rebound in the long run. The only way to end life and death's struggle is to heal the sick. Our cells will keep them alive 'til we can do that." His tone rises excitedly. "First, we use our Deathalyser, which they breathe into, so we can assess how many years they have left, then we—"

"Not now …" Mojo cuts in, touching his arm.

"Ah yes, of course, forgive me." He regains his train of thought. "No matter how much we try, our enemies keep hacking into our systems. When our terminal located you up top, those fiends saw it and got to you first."

I tense. "But we're safe for the moment, right?"

"Thanks to our defence shield," Mojo says gently. "They can't enter."

"For now," Cutter finishes bitterly.

Nausea hits, making me wince.

Mojo puts her hand on my shoulder once more. "You need to rest."

"Seems I've been resting for decades," I reply wearily. The world goes hazy. "All this dead talk's making me sick. There's got to be something bigger than …" The word rolls off my tongue. "Tomb-morrow."

Shadows sweep in, leaving me dead to the world.

My eyes open slowly.

The base's relentless humming sickens me. Its vibrations make me want to chuck. I can see why it's called the Regurgitator.

I look around. I'm in bed. The door nearby's shut.

My memories return. I cringe, then sit up, finding things less painful. The mark on my arm indicates an injection, no doubt to ease the pain. Whatever's gone in's worked.

Smoothly, I move out of bed, rise, and touch the humming door.

Locked, as expected.

I sigh, looking around the room, seeing only a dresser with three drawers. I pull the first two out, finding a few odds and ends. Not much, it seems.

I open the bottom one.

Jackpot.

A Terror-Wrist.

I pick it up, then stop. Why's it here? It's crucial to base security. Leaving it lying in a locked room for me to find so easily makes no sense. Putting it on and linking myself into the base, alerting everyone, even less so. Forget that.

A light flashes on its side. Static rises. Voices too. I lean in, listening. Hawkron, Mojo, Cutter and Spark are talking, meaning I'm in the loop, thanks to *their* wristbands. I keep listening, hoping like hell they don't find out.

Mojo speaks cautiously, *"Cutter, this isn't right ... "*

"Time's short," he shoots back. *"We've no choice."*

"Things could backfire," Spark warns. *"Badly."*

"The kid's useless," Cutter growls. *"We need Adam."*

My heart thumps. What the hell are they playing at?

Mojo breaks the silence. *"So what? We kill the kid and turn him back?"*

"Got any better ideas?"

I gasp, horrified.

"What was that?" Cutter snaps, having heard me through his wristband.

I tense, bracing for the worst.

"Who cares?" Mojo snaps back. *"Playing god's what's got us into this crap."*

"We're screwed if we don't," Cutter retorts. *"Put simply, genius, base power, draining. Bad guys, closing in. We do nothing, they win, and we get mindwiped, joining their ranks. Adam can fix this. He's the only one with psychic compatibility to ... "*

"EVE," Hawkron finishes.

A sharp breath rises.

Mojo.

"Too risky," she protests. *"We need a better way, Cutter ... "*

"I'm doing this, with or without you. Choose."

Silence. Then ...

"You're right," Spark relents. *"No choice. We'll grab the kid and get Adam back."*

"Hawkron?" Cutter presses, without a thought.

A long pause. Finally ...

"Yes indeed, Cutter. Our options are dead. I'm … in." His tone's calm. A little too calm. Like he's holding back.

Cutter doesn't notice. *"Mojo?"*

"Rot in hell!" she snaps.

His tone lowers. *"You going to be a problem? We can fix that."*

She gives another sharp breath, then submits. *"I'm in."*

"Great," comes the hard response.

"Yes," Hawkron agrees. *"We could use some good Mojo right about now."*

Beep!

My wristband.

More beeps rise from theirs.

"We've been hacked!" Cutter growls. *"What the f …?"*

Snap!

I rip the band from my arm, hurling it into the wall, killing it. I watch, shaken, as it drops onto the bed. I'm a dead guy walking. My life means nothing to them. Only Adam's. I'm meant to stay here, waiting for execution. Unless …

Another beep follows.

The door's sensor pad.

Instinct takes over. I grab the band off the bed, pressing a button. The band activates, but without the static, meaning no COM-Link. I step in, pressing it against the wallpad.

Click!

The door slides open with an automated hum. I step through, keeping hold of the band, knowing I'll need it to get around the base. They'll probably track it, but I've got no choice.

Footsteps rise in the adjacent corridor.

Voices follow. Cutter and Spark.

God, the meeting had been close by. I retreat, heading back along the passageway, turning a corner, and reaching a dead end. A door's on the left wall. It's shut. Locked too, no doubt. I place the band on its sensor pad and …

Hiss!

The door opens.

A storeroom's inside, filled with crates almost as big as me. I step in. The door hisses shut as I make for a shelf, grabbing a spanner. It's not much, fight-wise, but better than nothing.

A distant yell erupts. Cutter. He's found the room I've left. I frown, knowing the wristband was left for me on purpose, just not by him.

"How the hell'd he get out?" Cutter snaps.

"Must have had help," Spark replies.

"Get to the storeroom," Cutter orders. "Grab the Fire Drive. EVE'll need it. I'll change the base codes. He aint going anywhere."

"Right."

Cutter's footsteps clang off.

More footsteps follow, heading my way. I duck behind a crate, bracing myself. The door beeps, hissing open.

Spark steps in.

I clutch the spanner, tensing up. His shadow looms over me, growing larger. He looks my way then ...

I leap up, striking hard in a sweeping blur.

Clang!

He drops like a stone.

I grimace, hating what I've done, and hoping to god I haven't killed him. He'll return in another life anyway but still ...

I lean down, touching his neck. He's breathing, meaning there's still a Spark of life left in him.

I grab his wrist. A few tugs pull off his band. I drop it on a crate, smashing it with the spanner. The band flattens, wires bursting out. Another blow crushes it completely. With him and it down, I drop the spanner and back away, making for the door. Once in the corridor, I hit the sensor pad with my band.

The door hisses shut, locking.

I'm ready to run when the band magnetises to the screen. I let go and back off, ready for the worst. Instead, the screen flickers, bringing up a folder. The file opens, showing a map of the base's layout. The place is vast. Way bigger than I thought. Tech terms rise. Three words stick out.

Existential Vibrancy Enveloper.

EVE.

A light flickers on the map, highlighting a ventilation shaft near EVE, showing its gaseous overflow leading to the surface. A readout appears, saying how to switch those gases off. Another follows, stating that all cameras are disabled. This info, plus the wristband left for me in the drawer, indicates one thing.

No trap.

Since it can't be Cutter or Spark, it must be Hawkron or Mojo.

I reach in, pulling the wristband away, which detaches easily. I clutch it tightly before heading along the corridor, recalling the screen's path.

The lights dim to infrared.

Running footsteps rise in the distance. Doors slam shut. Loud clicks follow as the base goes into lockdown. Cutter must know what's happened. He's found Spark and returned to the Operations room.

I swear under my breath. I've spent too much time bypassing the locked doors and made a few wrong turns. I hurry down a flight of steps, reaching another sealed door. I raise the band, place it on the sensor pad, then …

Click!

The door slides open.

I step into a lab. Three metal coffins stand against the wall. A terminal hums before them. No, I realise. These aren't coffins. They're too big.

More like tombs.

Shimmering pipes from above, filled with multi-coloured streams, are plugged into them, humming softly.

I know what's inside.

A tough squeeze for a Corpmuscle.

Hawkron's words return. *"They're locked in the Incubators."*

"The what?" I'd pressed.

"Holding cells," he'd answered. *"Killing them means losing them, and they'll only rebound in the long run. The only way to end life and death's struggle is to heal the sick. Our cells will keep them alive 'til we can do that."*

Another door's opposite. Closed, and locked. The sensor pad shows that. I make for it, knowing it leads to EVE.

Flash!

I recoil as a shimmering pipe flares up, pumping power into the middle Incubator.

Hiss!

A high slit opens and two eyes peer out. They squint cruelly. A confident hiss follows, like whoever's in there's smiling.

"Ad-am!"

Their voice is husky.

Cautiously, I back away, making for the far door. They can't have opened the slit manually. They've had outside help, which means …

Beep!

The cell door whirrs, starting to open. A gloved hand emerges, pushing it outwards.

I reach the far door, hitting my band against its sensor pad.

Whirr!

The door slides open. I back out, watching the robed figure dive, lunging for the terminal. I hit my band against the outer wallpad, closing the door. The last thing I see before it shuts completely, is his fist slamming onto a button.

Whomp!

My heart sinks with the base's power generator, leaving only darkness.

"Oh, crap …" I whisper.

A whine follows from the back-up generator. I reach out, testing the door. It's locked, meaning he can't get to me, for now. I doubt he'll care. He'll be too interested in getting his blood-buddies into the base. What bugs me is who the hell let him out of his cell?

Then again, I was helped out of my room too.

I turn and hurry down the stairs, knowing this won't be the last time I'll be at death's door.

The stairway's long.

It takes time to reach the bottom. Finally, I arrive at a tunnel. Another door's nearby, this one open.

A hum comes from below.

EVE.

I'm sure of it.

I enter the doorway, descend another flight of stairs, then reach the chamber below. Rows of pipes and pressure valves stretch as far as I can see.

I head in further. The hum grows louder. I peer into the darkness and stop dead. Towering over everything, stands a giant metal sphere. Its thick alloy reminds me of the digital readouts I'd seen earlier.

EVE.

A terminal's before her. Flickering readings show she's active. Just. Thanks to her own generator.

The grilled floor squeaks behind me.

I whirl around, expecting the worst.

Hawkron.

He steps out of the darkness, bloodied and bruised. He collapses to his knees. The grills echo under his weight.

I swallow hard, not sure if I should help him or not.

"This your work?" I ask cautiously, wondering if he'd let the Corpmuscle out of his cell.

He coughs hard, indicating his wounds.

"I didn't do this to myself, my boy," he says wearily.

I nod. "How'd you get here?"

"Garbage chute," he answers. "Had to slide down it. Wasn't easy. Or pleasant." He seethes, frustrated by the thought. "I've sealed it shut. Laser cutter." He holds it up, then tosses it on a table. "Bloody thing's drained now."

"Where are the others?"

"Dead," he flat-out answers.

His reply hits me like a bullet.

"What ...?" I whisper.

He shakes his head "Mojo was always too soft." He glances at my wristband. "She left that for you to find. Once you were up and running, she sent you the info to reach EVE."

"So what happened?" I ask, ready for a mother of a smackdown.

He continues. "She, more than any of us, wanted this to be over. She was simply burnt out. She loved you – my apologies – loved Adam, more than anything." He winces painfully. "I'd gone with Cutter in word only. He was beyond reason. Mojo and I were at the terminal in the Operation's room when he ran in and saw her screen, showing you in the Incubation chamber. Her readouts showed she'd been helping you. He pushed her away and hit a switch, freeing the Corpmuscle to kill you." He winces again. "She hit the wall and pulled out her gun. He was already armed and they fired. Bullets rebounded, one nipping my shoulder." He indicates his wound. "They kept firing, until hitting each other. His head was blown apart while she fell onto the terminal, seeing you flee the Corpmuscle. She watched as you sealed the chamber door, saving yourself, right before he took out the base's power. Her last act was to bring our energy reserves back online."

I look around. "Just the lights and oxygen?"

"COM Links too," he adds. "All doors can be slid open manually, meaning the rest of his bloody Corpmuscles can flow in. At least he won't be able to bypass our back-up systems, nor power the base up again. I've seen to that."

I nod. "What about Spark?"

He sighs. "Our Corpmuscle got to him, leaving one bloody big mess."

I shudder. "But we've still got EVE. She's on her own generator."

"Yes, but she's not fully operational," comes the reply. "Adam only used her prototype to draw people back from the dead. Once he was gone, we worked tirelessly on EVE. Constructing her took decades, and she's still not ready. Her ability to heal's not fully functional. Thanks to Cutter, her power to eradicate, is."

I tense, taking this in. "You mean wiping higher powers from existence?"

No reply.

"Oh, you are kidding me ..."

"Life's no joke," he says back.

"So what are we s'posed to do?" I retort. "Sit here and wait for the bowels of hell to flood from Satan's infected colon? EVE's our only way out of this crap. Life's one big gamble and we need the upper hand."

He smiles. "Your idealism hasn't changed, Adam. You never wanted EVE to destroy, only to heal. To you, she was short for, in your words, *Eve*olution!"

"God almighty."

"That's what we're playing." He draws a sharp breath. "All or nothing, it seems. That's existence after all."

He staggers up.

I help him to the terminal and we get to work.

Clang!
Clang!
Clang!

Footsteps on the stairs.

Hawkron and I look up from the terminal. Two Corpmuscles are descending the long stairway, leading a third figure.

Varkos.

They're early.

"Unholy crap," I whisper, filled with dread.

We're not finished. EVE's working too slowly. Her energy's draining, along with the base's power, meaning we'd no alerts of the Corpmuscles breaking in.

We duck behind the terminal. Hawkron pulls out a gun. I go to grab it. He pulls it away.

"Better let me," he says. "I was a crack shot in the marines."

"Where'd you get that from?" I ask. "Cutter?"

"Cutter," he confirms.

The Corpmuscles near the floor.

Bang!

Hawkron's shot's bang on target. The bullet thuds under one of their hoods, making their head arch back in a bloodied burst. He fires again, sending the second Corpmuscle reeling in the same bloody way. They tumble down the stairs, landing in a heap on the floor. He aims at Varkos and fires. Varkos ducks, scampers down the stairs and leaps, taking cover behind a crate.

Hawkron re-aims.

Varkos leaps up, firing at Hawkron who fires back. They both duck, dodging each other's shots.

More Corpmuscles appear at the top of the stairs.

Hawkron aims again.

Click!

He ducks swiftly.

"Damn," he grimaces. "I'm out."

Screech!

Piercing metal erupts from the nearby lift shaft. A shuffle follows as a small, shadowy shape crawls out. I note the shaft. Hawkron had come in via a garbage chute. This shaft's so tight that only a kid could've come down it.

I tense.

"Is that ...?" I begin.

"Yes," he replies gravely. "The Ex-Terminated."

Another screech erupts, this one beastly.

His face hardens. "Varkos and his lot were driving our fire, giving their boss time to crawl in."

I peer into the shadows. "He's that small?"

"Indeed," he answers, "and it's not a he, but a she."

"They're female?" I ask, baffled.

"Not only that," he says grimly. "She was–"

"Don't tell me …" I cringe.

"Your wife," he finishes.

My jaw drops.

"The one you killed," he adds. "Which is why she's so bitter. She's your ex. Terminated."

I stare at him, shocked. "What about Mojo? Hadn't I hooked up with her?"

"On the side," he answers.

"So I was fooling around with her while I had a dying wife and raising the dead? That's sick!"

"Not as sick as the karmic seeds you planted," he corrects. "Everything here's from the fruits of your labour."

They rise, stepping into the blood-red light, glaring at me.

I want to hurl.

Their skin's dark. Scaly. Their nose, long and pointed. Their ears, larger than their head. Their mouldy teeth, razor-sharp, while their lips are burnt, black and charred. They step in, raising a rusty pipe, ready to strike.

I tense to run.

They're faster, sweeping in, grabbing me by the throat, pulling me down and bringing their repulsive features up to mine. Their hot nauseating breath sears my face as they jab a cold, jagged pipe end under my chin, pushing my head up. Long streams of mucous and saliva drip from her nose and mouth, dribbling thickly down her jaw. Her head rises cruelly as she snarls in a crackly voice, "Karma's a bitch!"

I'm ready to chuck.

"You forgot to give me a goodbye kiss … darling!" She scowls, disgusted. "The kiss of life, my love. We both know it sucks, big time." Her deformed eyes dart up to EVE, then back again. "Adam, EVE, and the apple of your eye." She twists the pipe harder into my chin, glancing at the rusted metal. "Do you know … what this is … darling?"

I stare at her, too terrified to breathe.

"This is the rod *you* told me to trust in. The rod *you* said would bring me back to my body. The rod that failed. Do you know what I call it now?" She sneers cruelly. "The raw end of the stick!" She jabs my head up with it. "Who gave you the right to *terminate* our relationship?"

I swallow hard. "I–"

She shrieks fiercely.

Smack!

My eyes flash as I hit the ground, my cheek burning from the rod's savage strike. She shrieks again, booting me in the stomach. I roll over in agony, feeling the floor's icy grilles pressed against my bloodied face.

"*Don't* talk!" she hisses. "I've been to hell and back 'cause of you, Sam Silver. You owe me a great deal. I call it …" Her slimy lips curl up as she sneers, "… Hellimoney!"

She boots me again, then strikes hard. I wail in agony, my shoulder searing. She raises the rod high, shrieking louder than ever, before belting my forehead savagely. I howl as she tenses fiercely, then …

Bang!

She stops in her tracks.

Hawkron. His gun reloaded.

The bullet ricochets away. A warning shot, I realise. Killing her would mean stalling the war, not ending it.

He speaks darkly. "It's been a long time … Roller."

She flinches at the name. Her face falls as she gazes sorrowfully at him. Shades of hurt rise from below her psychotic storm, exposing her pain. She may look like a psycho dwarf from a nightmare fairytale, but her eyes tell a different story. If anything she's … human.

I focus on what Hawkron's said.

"Roller?" I ask gently.

She steps back, sadly.

"Ebony Roller," he presses, talking to her as much as me. "That's her name. Her *real* name."

"Fitting," I grimace. "She's life and death rolled into one."

Click!

Varkos. His gun's aimed at Hawkron.

Hawkron doesn't budge, keeping his own gun fixed on her. "We can fix this, Roller. Together." He stares deep into her eyes. "We know what you want. What you *truly* want. What you've always wanted, even as a little girl, long before any of this started." His voice softens. "To find your place. To … fit in."

She flinches again, trembling.

I glance at Varkos. His face is hard. Cruel. Ruthless. He won't ally with anyone, that's for sure.

Beep!

The terminal screen changes. I look up, seeing the sequence Hawkron keyed in earlier. It was slow in activating, care of the base's power drain. Now, it's finally here.

EVE's activation codes.

All we need is to hit enter, and she'll come to life. There's less than a minute to do it, or the system'll go back several steps, blocking us out. It's now or never.

"Roller …" Hawkron presses.

Varkos's gun arm tenses.

I lunge, wrenching the rod from her clawed hand. She screeches as I roll over, hurling the rod at Varkos.

Bang!

Hawkron cries out and falls against the terminal, clutching his side.

Smack!

Varkos recoils as the rod strikes his chest, rebounds and hits the terminal keypad. A hum rises before another shot follows, this one from Hawkron. Varkos falls back, his throat bursting into a bloody mass where the bullet's struck him head-on. Both he and Hawkron drop like stones. Hawkron's arm flails sideways, sending the rod rolling back to me.

The Ex-Terminated leaps, shrieking wildly, striking me hard, picking up the rod and thrusting it into my neck, crushing my breath. I push back fiercely. She's too strong and we roll over in a heap.

Several Corpmuscles sweep down the stairway.

Hawkron pushes himself up weakly, firing repeatedly. Each shot's dead-on, sending the Corpmuscles rolling down the stairs, landing in a heap. Only one's left, peering out from the door at the top of the stairway, not daring to descend.

The Ex-Terminated snarls, drops the rod and falls onto my neck, guzzling hungrily, releasing thick blood streams. I scream wildly, convulsing in agony, as she rises. She licks my blood off her lips, sending it dripping onto my face, smearing it, then sneers repulsively. "Now you see what it's like … to be bled dry."

I hiss back, enraged. "Get a life and stop sucking off mine!"

A mechanised whine rises.

EVE.

She's online.

The Ex-Terminated looks up, horrified. "No …!"

I grab the rod from the ground and–

Smack!

Her head arches sideways from my blow, spitting out a mixture of blood and saliva as she falls away. I push myself up and scramble back, clutching my bleeding neck. I look at Hawkron. He's slumped against the terminal, far worse than me.

The Ex-Terminated screeches, diving for me. I raise the rod, smacking her back again. She hits a railing. I retreat, scrambling through chunks of her blood and saliva. My hand slides on a chunky lump, I slip, hit the grilles, she dives and–

Squelch!

She gawps in horror as her black, sloppy slime spills over me. I stare back at her, shocked. My hand quivers as her insides flood out, drenching me. Her eyes droop as she slumps to her knees, looking down to where the rod's protruding from.

"Trust you," she whispers, "to break my heart." A final choke hurks up a slime ball, then she hits the grilles, dead to the world.

I shudder, sick as hell, watching her insides drain away.

EVE's hum grows louder.

I roll over. The slop drips off me as I look up, seeing Hawkron. His eyes are barely open as he speaks croakily, but relieved.

"At last," he murmurs. "All I ever wanted … was for this to be over for good … and evil."

His head rolls sideways, lying still.

EVE's hum grows into a high-pitched whine, then …

Snap!

A pipe-like hatch, near her base, flips open.

Flash!

A blinding white light shoots out, covering Hawkron. I shield my eyes from its blazing glow, then blink hard, peering through it. His body's convulsing. Jerking awkwardly. His head rises, his jaw opens and I watch, astounded, as he exhales a bright green mist.

The core of his very being, I conclude.

His lifeforce.

His soul.

The cloud rises a little, then stops in mid-air, hovering. Twisting. Wavering.

EVE tingles gently, enveloping in her glow, drawing him in. He bristles brighter than ever, more than happy to follow her lead. Steadily, he moves in, picking up speed before shooting into the pipe, sweeping down it and vanishing from sight.

As part of what I call, an EVE-vent.

EVE's glow strikes me too. I shut my eyes, shielding them from her blinding spark. It doesn't help. She's too strong for that. My temples tingle as my heart pounds, elated, ready to burst from my chest and surge ahead.

A clang comes from the stairway.

The final Corpmuscle.

I pull myself back to reality and wrench free of the glow, refusing to get sucked in by anything. Common sense brings me down to earth as I roll away, taking cover behind a crate.

EVE bristles with a high resonance. Her beam refocuses, hitting the Ex-Terminated's mutated corpse in its heavenly aura. The carcass sizzles, before its vile head splits open, releasing a thick black cloud, dripping with ethereal sludge.

EVE growls furiously, dragging the sick deathforce in for her EVE-vent. The cloud resists her pull, refusing to lighten up, but the attempt's futile. Slowly, it's sucked into the long vent. The vent rumbles, compressing it heavily, before pulling the Ex-Terminated out of this world.

EVE's whine softens and her glow flickers, absorbing the putrid essence. A gurgle, then a belch, follows, releasing a puff of white steam. EVE's whine and glow dim, before suddenly rising again, her power restored. Her beam darts over the chamber, scanning the place like an eye seeking a target. Finally, it shoots to the stairs, before targeting another corpse, then engulfing it. Another black cloud's wrenched out, but nowhere near as heavy.

Varkos.

She pulls hard.

Whoosh!

He sweeps into the vent. Gurgles follow, like he's hard to digest. The beam dims again, though not as bad, then strengthens. The chamber's scanned rapidly, before several more shadows are grabbed.

Corpuscles.

They too, are drawn into the EVE-vent, vanishing from sight.

EVE's scan soars high, penetrating the thick walls. Her beam soon re-tracts, bearing three clouds, much lighter.

Mojo, Spark, and Cutter.

Cutter's no doubt the black one. Mojo's gold, which stands to reason. As for the other–

"Hmmm," I muse "Seems he really was a bright Spark after all."

All three shoot into EVE.

Her beam reaches for me again. I dodge it and lunge for the terminal, hitting the digital keyboard. Her glow flickers, then wavers. A mechanised shrill, like a cry, echoes piercingly through the chamber. I recoil, covering my ears, as her glow dims, retracts into the EVE-vent, zips in and then …

Snap!

The hatch slams shut.

EVE's whine lowers, turning into a hum, before fading completely.

Silence follows.

It's over.

I rest wearily on the terminal, shaking my head. EVE's heavenly residue tingles, along with the Ex-Terminated's sick stench. I look at EVE sadly. Light and dark, heaven and hell, they're all cramped into EVE as a giant, swirling mass. Then again, I reason, isn't that the same for all of us?

The terminal beeps. Readings appear on the screen. I analyse them curi-ously. EVE's impervious to attack. Resistant to digital and physical entry. Nothing she's consumed can escape. They'll be contained for a century or so, meaning they're prisoners. For now.

At least until I can find a cure for them all.

Two digital buttons appear. One grey. One red.

Containment.

Vaporisation.

I frown, astounded. That's it? What about healing? Curing people for the greater good? That was Adam's vision. Where's that option?

I hit a few switches, searching for it, but find nothing. I sigh, frustrated. Maybe Adam wasn't around long enough to set that up. He knew that healing takes time, so things had to be done right. Getting sick's easy. Wellness takes effort. A *lot* of effort. So why didn't Hawkron and the rest work that into the system? They had decades. More than enough time. I think hard. Finally, the truth hits home.

Cutter. The hazy grey Cutter through light and dark.

He sabotaged EVE. He was too arrogant, to think he'd end up in there himself. He could never be a healer. How could he? He'd too much anger.

I hit the keyboard. A blip follows and I step back. EVE and everyone inside her's sealed. For now.

I study the screen, then peer in, astonished. The readings are starting to make sense. I can understand them. Most of them anyway. My excitement grows. Given time, a *long* time, I can learn the rest and operate EVE, meaning I can carry out Adam's vision. Granted, it'll be damn near impossible to heal the Ex-Terminated and his sick lot, but I'm up for it. I can do this, I'm sure. I sigh, relieved, knowing that healing's ahead, for all of us. The war's over. Finally over …

A shadow falls.

I whirl around, seeing a sword's hilt sweep in.

Flash!

I'm struck heavily, crying out from the gashing strike to my forehead. I fall over the terminal before slumping to the floor, hitting the grilles. My vision blurs as a hand reaches for me.

Belonging to a Corpmuscle.

My throat's clasped.

I lie helplessly at the terminal's base as their grip tightens. Behind me, EVE's hum morphs into a whine, as if sensing my pain, knowing the worst is to come.

Her tension's boiling over.

In a final scream of terminal madness.

Damn me to hell.

Every tale's too close to call. Or should that be *tail?* Yeah, that'd be right. Choosing the wrong one'll only summon a hell-hound, leaving me with a real bitch of a problem.

Namely, Meridian. I can hear them, crackling through the speaker, almost in joy.

I grab the final lot of papers.

One story left. Maybe they're saving the *beast* 'til last.

I pick them up, almost knowing what to expect. Then again, I reason, there's always surprises.

Nasty ones.

Chapter Six

Hell's Belle's

Scalpehill's a death trap.

I was warned to stay away from there as a kid. Even in high school, we knew better than to go near it. A few friends even worked their butts off so they wouldn't have to live there one day. The whole suburb's feral.

I tense, turning the car off the main road into a long, winding street. Rundown houses are to the left. A park's to the right. At the end of the park's a council housing estate. A lone block of a building, bleak, grimy, and several storeys high. We've always called it the Flats, care of the sheer number of roof-jumpers who end up flat on the ground. The estate has it all. Drugs, murders, suicides, the works.

A small group of people meamble down the street to the bus stop. Their faces are long and drawn. Their eyes, sunken. Their clothes, disgusting. They see me driving past and raise their arms, yelling angrily. God knows why. I can't get away fast enough.

The street curves around and they vanish from sight. I drive a short way, before reaching the place I'm looking for. A townhouse. Sure, it needs work, but seems better than the housing estate opposite. Almost passable.

Belle, short for Belinda, and I have been friends since high school. Best buds. Nothing romantic's ever happened. We've never even thought about it. The whole guy/girl thing's not an issue with us. We just love to hang out. Where we differ is that she's got a better job, earning much more than me, which is how she got this place. She said she wanted to start small. I told her there's a difference between small and bottom of the barrel. She just laughed and shrugged it off, the dreamer as always. The whole area's going up, she'd said. Slowly, but getting there. When her townhouse reaches a suitable value, she'll sell it off. She invited me over the second it was in her name. She's over the moon. Anyone else'd be freaked.

I pull into her driveway, stop the car and get out, rising into the chilly air. A cold breeze wafts by, like it's risen from a chasm.

The front door opens, and she emerges, grinning eagerly. "Hey, dude! Welcome to Le Chateau Belle! Like it?"

I nod back.

"Nice," is all I can say.

She laughs. "Yeah right. You saw the Flats and freaked, didn't you?"

"I ..."

"Right?"

I indicate the house. "Well, it's a start."

"Prude!" She laughs again. "Relax, it's not that bad."

Cries rise from down the street. The dazed mob's rounding the bend, heading our way. I know they'll blow at the sight of me.

"Uh, why don't you show me inside?" I ask quickly.

"Love to," she says. She grins cheekily. "I know you're dying to see it."

The place is small. Cramped too. The kitchen, laundry and living room are all on the ground floor, while the bedroom, shower and bath's upstairs. The paintwork's faded. Belle's more than happy to fix it. Even talking about it gives her a buzz. She's excited, unlike the dazed mob outside. I see them from the downstairs window. They're so spaced-out they don't even notice my car, thank god. Dully, they saunter away, heading 'round another bend, engrossed in their little world.

We head upstairs. She shows me her room, then the spare one opposite.

"And this ..." she says, pushing the squeaking door in, "is yours."

"For what?" I ask baffled. "A place to crash?"

"Uh ... no," she corrects. "More than that."

I stare at her, cautiously. "What do you mean?"

She grins again.

I know that face. I've seen it too many times. "Oh no! No, no, no! You've screwed up again, haven't you? You need the money ..."

She raises her hand. "I may have misjudged things a little …"

"… So you need a flatmate?" I finish.

Silence.

"Well?" I press.

More silence.

"You so do," I push.

She relents and nods. "Uh-huh. Yeah."

"Here? No way!" I turn to leave.

She puts her arm against the wall, blocking me off. "Rent's dirt cheap. Pretty much zilch. Hey, you're always telling me you hate where you're living."

"Not that much." I look out the bedroom window at the Flats across the street and cringe. They seem like Dracula's castle.

She presses on. "Come on dude, I need a little help for a month. Just *one* month, I swear. I'll be fine once I'm up and running, but I'm desperate right now. Anyway, I've saved your butt enough times, remember?"

"Really?" I retort.

"Yeah. The Montanna Demon?"

I inhale sharply, recalling that high-school hell-diva. The girl's real name was Montanna Devon. She screwed me over, big time.

"You owe me for that," Belle warns.

I sigh wearily. "I don't know, B."

"Fine, I'll give the old MD a call." She pulls out her phone. "Last chance, buddy. I'm warnin' ya …"

I raise my hand. "Hold it …'

Her eyes light up. "Be a roomie and we'll forget about it." She puts the phone on a table, then grabs my shoulders, staring straight at me. "The whole world sucks but we've always bailed each other out. We're a *team*." She squeezes my shoulders tightly. "We've travelled together, man. This'll be the same. Won't it?"

"I—"

"Trust me, there'll be no problems, I swear. You're clean. Not fussy or a slob. Everything'll be fifty-fifty." She shakes me back and forth. "It'll be *so good*! Freedom man, freedom!" She stares deep into my eyes, full of life, with that infectious grin of hers.

I sigh again, knowing there's no way I can say no, but won't tell her that. Not straight away.

"Let me think about it," I say. "I'll tell you in the morning."

"Morning hell, let's talk over a snack. Fridge is full."

"Belle ..."

"Come on ..."

She turns me around, pushing me downstairs.

I go home, disgruntled.

Belle's been convincing, but she's right. I'm so over where I'm renting, due to psycho Mrs. Turner next door. Now *there's* a nutjob who belongs in the Flats. Or a hospital at least. The old bag's more unhinged than my back gate.

Belle knows this well. I've whinged about Mrs. Turner a lot. I barely get home when Belle bugs me with a text, saying her offer'll give me an excuse to ditch the bitch. I turn my phone off but get no peace. Mrs. Turner comes right over, more nuts than ever. I can usually take her, but not after the Flats. She bangs on my door, screaming for me to keep the noise down. I'm only playing a soft song for god's sake. She bangs the door harder. I could call the cops but no. I need out and fast.

Screw it, I conclude, riled to hell. I'll move in with Belle. Between Mrs. Turner and the Montanna Demon, I've no choice. I'd be crazy to stay where I am.

Then again, going by where Belle lives, there's no escaping crazy.

I drive up her street once more, now with my car packed to the hilt. Belle was over the moon when I grumpily took her offer. A little *too* excited. Why, I don't know. I've never seen her like this. Unless she's in more trouble than she's let on.

Strangely, for all her joy, she's not there when I arrive. I find the hidden key she's told me about and open the front door, grateful that no loudmouths are walking by today. I unpack the car, hating every moment. It's not so much the suburb this time. It's more from walking up the sloping driveway, then a long flight of stairs, carrying my stuff to my room, before going back and forth to my car. For some reason, the house feels colder now.

Belle comes home a few hours later, naturally when I've unpacked everything. I'm sure she's skived off.

"Sam!" she beams, entering with a pizza. "This is so cool!"

I shiver, feeling the cold. "Sure is."

She puts the pizza down and leans in, hugging me. "Any probs, let me know. This is all two-way. We can talk anything, and I mean *anything*, over. No fights, okay?"

"Sure."

She glances at the stairs. "Just watch the bottom step, hey? Need to get that fixed."

"No problem." I look at the pizza. "Wanna give me a slice? I'm starving."

"All yours. Let's chuck on a film too."

"You're on."

Pizza and a movie, total heaven.

The world falls away as we laugh like never before. The show finishes and we talk long into the night, firing up our dreams against the world, making plans for well into the future. There's no Mrs. Turner. No Flats. No loudmouths. No chilling winds. Just us. Relaxed to the max.

Total bliss.

Finally, we go to bed. We make quips across the hall from our rooms until, at last, there's silence. The joy of the night fades away, leaving only the Flats, looming through my bedroom window. I don't care. I'm too blissed out for that.

I put the radio on to distract myself. Soon, I'm dead to the world.

My dreams are vivid.

Everything's so clear. It's just like being awake.

I stand in a surreal landscape, watching the glistening dewdrops on the grass. Crickets chirp loudly. Birds sing from the gently rustling leaves of a great oak. A warm wind breezes past. It's like I'm linked, *really* linked, into another realm.

I should be in heaven, but no. There's a glitch. I can sense it.

I look into the distance. Heavy black storm clouds loom on the horizon.

I frown, confused.

"Storm's coming," a nearby voice says.

I turn and see my old science teacher, Mister Nero, standing with a group of people. They're all family and friends. Many have long since died.

I stare at them, astounded.

"What are they doing here?" I find myself asking him.

"We came to see you," he replies. *"It's been a long time."*

117

Without knowing what I'm saying, I ask, *"It's coming, isn't it?"*

"Cakes?" a woman asks. She walks by, holding two large sponge cakes. There's no plates and they crumble between her fingers.

I keep my focus on Mister Nero, asking, *"How long?"*

His gaze hardens, like he's staring right through me. *"Try and touch that tree."*

I reach for the trunk. An unseen force pushes back. I can't get to it, no matter how I try.

I step back, astounded.

"I can't," I whisper.

"That," he says, *"is what you must beware of."*

Bang!

My eyes snap open as my bedroom door slams shut. I sit up, shaking. A storm's outside. Streaks of lightning illuminate the Flats. A thunderclap booms, then an icy breeze chills me to the bone. I look over. My window's partly open. I shiver, knowing I'd locked it earlier.

The staircase near my room creaks heavily.

Footsteps.

Going down it.

"Belle?" I call, sitting up.

Slowly, I rise out of bed, make my way to the door and touch the handle. The door opens with a long, drawn-out squeak.

I peer into the corridor. Belle's door's ajar. She's probably getting a glass of water. Strange that she hasn't yelled out about my door slamming shut. That's not like her. Ah, who cares?

I shut the door, go to the window and lock it. When it's secure, I get into bed, turn on the lamp, and put on the radio, hearing the soft flow of classical night music.

Outside, the rain hammers down.

I go back to sleep, falling into a long, dreamless slumber. There's no visions, sounds, feelings, nothing. Only darkness.

I awake, feeling like no time's passed at all. Memories surface, making me feel icky. The dreams, the open window, the door slamming, I knew this place was nuts from the word go.

I get out of bed and go downstairs for breakfast. When I reach the kitchen, Belle's looking into the fridge, frustrated.

"Morning," I say wearily.

She turns to me angrily, pointing at the fridge. "Did you eat our pizza?"

"Why would I do that?" I ask back. "We always have cold brekky leftovers."

She glares at me. "I'll ask again, did you eat it?"

"No," I retort. "I didn't come down here last night."

Her face hardens. "Don't lie!"

"I'm not lying."

"I heard you on the stairs!"

"Hey," I shoot back. "*You* came downstairs. Not me!"

She ignores me. "I was saving it for lunch today. Now I got nothing. Thanks, Sam! Thanks, heaps!"

She slams the fridge door and storms off.

I make a face. "Any probs, let me know," I mimic. "This is all two-way. We can talk about anything. No fights, okay?"

I shake my head and open the fridge door.

She's right. The pizza's gone, including the box.

"What the hell ...?" I murmur. I'd heard her on the stairs last night. Hadn't I?

I stop, then frown.

No, I reason, I hadn't seen *her*, but even that doesn't make sense. Why would anyone break in, sneak downstairs and steal our pizza?

I shut the fridge door and head for the cereal box, swearing to ditch this place ASAP and find somewhere psycho-free.

Knowing my luck, it won't be easy.

Belle leaves for work soon after, leaving me to settle in. I write five pages of my next novel but can't focus. The clock ticks loudly on the wall. I hate that clock. I can't think with its echo bouncing off the walls, not that I *can* think much in this place.

Sighing, I drop my pad onto the couch. I'm going for a walk.

A police siren wails outside.

"Crap."

Who cares, I vow. I'm off.

"Stay back!"

The cop raises his hands, blocking off a group of people from the Flats. Two more cops kneel behind him, placing a blanket over a body. Horrified murmurs grow as an ambulance drives up.

I retreat shakily.

"Oh dear," a voice says glumly from behind me. "Another one."

I stop and look back. An elderly lady's in my way. She steps around me, staring ahead.

"Another one?" I ask.

"A jumper," she says back. "Off the roof. Another '*flatmate*' for all of us."

I gulp sickly.

"More frequently these days," she continues. "It's this place, y'know. It sends people crazy." She looks at me curiously. "You're new here, aren't you? You're not caught up in things yet." She shakes her head. "You'd best leave while you can. Before it's too late."

She lowers her head sadly, turns and walks away.

I shiver. Screw Belle's big dreams about her first house. Things are rapidly worsening. I need out and fast.

Time to start looking.

Ruffled, I turn and head off.

There's no luck finding anything online. At least not cheaply. I search on and off during the day until finally, around dinner time, I toss my laptop sideways onto the couch and give a big yawn and stretch. Moments later, Belle comes through the door, much brighter than this morning.

"Hey dude," she says, throwing her bag on the couch. "Sorry 'bout before, hey? Look, I don't know what happened last night, or who ate what, but we can fix things, right?"

I nod warily. "Sure."

"Cheers." She yawns. "God I'm tired. I'm off to bed."

I glance at the clock. "Already? You serious?"

"Yeah."

"It's only six."

"Yeah, but I work hard. See you in the morning, dude."

I frown, confused. "Right."

She gives a long stretch and heads upstairs.

My dreams are normal again. Nothing freaky this time, save for a pump-kin-headed priest. I'm sky dancing with them when …

Crash!

My eyes snap open.

A plate's smashed in the kitchen.

Probably Belle.

Another plate smashes, then another, then another.

I sit up quickly, wondering what the hell's going on. Is Belle going nuts again or …

The crashing grows louder.

No choice.

I rub my eyes, get out of bed, open my bedroom door, look into the corridor and see Belle's door open.

I move over and peer in.

Her bed's full.

Crash!

Another plate.

I shudder.

An icy wind sweeps over my face. Belle's window's open. I stare at her bed, astounded. How the hell can she sleep through this? What …?

Whoosh!

A wind gust sweeps in from her window. I recoil, then …

Bang!

Her door slams shut.

I grab the handle and twist hard.

Locked.

I try a few more times.

Nothing.

"Belle!" I whisper, hitting the door. "Belle!"

I push my shoulder into it. No luck.

Crap.

I look to my bedroom and gulp. No phone. I'd left it charging downstairs.

Double crap.

No choice.

Holding my breath, I slowly make for the stairs. The wooden steps creak under my weight.

Squeaking taps come from below.

The back door's open.

Mumbling rises from the kitchen. Cupboard doors open and shut rapidly as pots and pans are overturned.

Defying gut instincts, I creep on. Finally, I reach the second last step. I step down, the plank gives way and I trip and fall, hitting the front door.

The banging in the kitchen stops dead.

Running footsteps sweep through the dark.

I leap up and grab a vase from the bookshelf, ready to hurl it.

A screech erupts as the shadowy figure retreats, scurrying under the stairway, cowering in fright. Whimpers follow, then a scratchy voice speaks. "Hide and seek, hide and seek. Must hides. Must hides!"

I reach for the light switch.

"Noooooo!" the voice screeches. "Torch fires! Hurtses!" Gurgling chokes erupt. "Blooddrops fly in the storm! Nevermore be a safe path."

I gulp. This is way too close to my dream.

I reach for the light switch again.

A cry erupts as they leap out from under the stairs, grab the coffee table and wrench it up, aiming for me. I recoil into the wall as it falls past, slamming onto the floor, then watch as the freak grabs my phone, scurries into the kitchen on all fours and makes for the back door screaming, "Too soon! Too soon!"

I scramble up and run after them.

They make it to the laundry, dart outside, then turn back, grabbing the door handle.

With a muddy hand.

A muddy *human* hand.

Bang!

The door slams shut.

I run over, bolt it, and peer through the window into the small backyard.

There's no sign of them.

I back away, shaken.

My leg hits a bucket, knocking it over. I jump, boot it sideways and retreat into the kitchen, freaking at every shadow. I shudder as I stumble into the living room. Panic takes over and I bolt for the stairs, leap over the broken step and fly for Belle's room. Finally, I reach the top, grab the cold door handle and twist hard.

The door shoots open.

"Belle!"

Thump, thump, thump!

Footsteps. Running across the floor. "Can't be found, can't be found …"

My heart leaps as I hit the light switch. A flash ignites, then my eyes adjust, expecting the worst.

Strangely, everything's normal. Sure it's a mess, as always, but there's no sign of any gremlins. The wardrobe's open and I can see under the bed. There's just Belle, lying in it, dead to the world.

I run over, shaking her. "Belle! *Belle!* Wake the hell up!"

She groans sleepily and opens her eyes. "Turn the light off and make sure the door hits your butt on the way out."

She rolls over.

"Hey!" I snap, shaking her again. "We gotta leave! Now! We're not safe!"

She shoves me away. "Dude, I've got an early start. Go back to bed and think of porn or something."

I grab her arm, pulling her up. "Move!"

She growls as rage takes over, then leaps out of bed, shoving me to the door. "Get-out-of-my-face!"

She whirls me around, throws me into the corridor, then slams the door, locking it.

I kick it furiously.

"Screw you!" I roar. "I'm outta here you dumb bi–!"

I kick it harder. The door shakes violently as I turn, bolt downstairs and leap over the broken step. Stuff the cow. I'm ditching this dump. Fast.

I snatch my car keys off the bench and make for the front door. I'm almost there when I stop dead. There's grime on my shirt. A small patch of dirt. Like soil from the backyard.

Where'd the hell that come from? I haven't been outside.

Forget it. I'm gone.

I reach the front door.

A glimmer in the window catches my eye. I peek through the curtains, peer outside, and freeze.

Frozen beyond words.

Several people are in the street dancing dreamily, blissfully, hazily. An old woman twirls in the middle of the road. She's the one I'd met earlier at the Flats. She's barefoot and in a long, white nightie. A pale-faced man with short brown hair's nearby. He's juggling steak knives. A young woman goes past him, riding a unicycle. An older man follows, leaping up and down like an ape. He turns, leaps up onto the footpath and sniffs the grass.

More people appear. A large man with a bushy moustache leads them. He's wearing a white short-sleeved shirt, butcher's apron, and holds two meat cleavers. He chops maniacally, slicing at invisible chunks. A cowboy trails, carrying two hand-held drills, firing them like guns. A clown dances by, holding two flaming torches. He raises one to his mouth to eat it while turning his eyes towards me.

I duck out of sight, petrified. My phone's gone. There's no landline. My laptop's dead, killing any chance of calling for help. My heart pounds. I can't see any options. What do I do? What the hell do I do?

The old lady's words return. *"It's this place, y'know. It sends people crazy."*

Now she's twirling in the street, reaching for the full moon.

Her voice grows louder in my mind. *"You're new here, aren't you? You're not caught up in things yet. You'd best leave while you can. Before it's too late."*

" ... too late."

" ... too late."

" ... too late."

The clock strikes midnight.

I jump, struggling to hold what's left of my sanity. Is this even real? Or is it me? Am I the one who's nuts here? I can't be, can I?

Her words grow louder than ever.

"It sends people crazy."

" ... Crazy."

" ... Crazy."

" ... Crazy."

Sweat trickles down my face as I lie frozen, staring up at the window, not knowing what's real and what's not. The clock ticks louder than ever. Each tick's like a knife to the heart. My hands shake. My mouth's dry. I'm too scared to breathe. I tremble, terrified by the insane chuckles from outside, taunting me into the darkness.

Slowly, I melt into the shadows, too scared to move.

Sunbeams seep through the blinds, touching my cheek. I blink, finding myself by the window. The street freaks are still outside, I can hear them, but their madness is fading, dispelled by the rising sun. Finally, they vanish completely, leaving only silence.

I'm too shocked to move.

Belle's bedroom door opens. She yawns groggily as she comes down the stairs, ignoring the broken step and her trashed living room. I swallow hard and sit up. Shakily, I pull myself onto the couch as she walks sleepily over to the sink, looks in, then explodes.

"What the f …?" she cries, throwing an arm up. "What the hell's this? You're s'posed to clean up! If you wanna live here man, you gotta follow rules! Look at it!"

I stare at her, astounded.

"Look!" she roars. "Biscuit crumbs on the sink! Two of them! Two damn crumbs! Screw you!" She grabs the frying pan, hurling it at the window.

Smash!

The glass splits and the pan clangs noisily to the floor. "I'm sick of it! Sick because *you*, you tosser, aren't pulling your weight! Thanks heaps! Loser!"

She boots the overturned table, storms to the stairs, ignores the broken step once more, stomps back up to her room and slams the door shut with a resounding bang.

I jump, then glance outside.

No sign of anyone.

Screw this, I'm outta here.

Flying into overdrive, I grab my car keys and bolt out the door.

My mind tingles as I drive away. The further from the Flats I go, the more my head clears, like whatever's back there's falling away.

Or I'm waking up.

Doesn't matter, I'm safe in my car. I drive around the bend that leads to the main road, relieved. No one can reach me. I've no idea what to do, where to go, or who'd believe me, but I'm free. My stuff can stay at Belle's place, I don't care, she can keep it, but I'm never going back. No way in hell. I'm finally, finally–

–being flagged down by a cop in the middle of the street. A patrol car blocks the road ahead. Another cop's nearby. I tense warily, unsure of anything right now.

I stop the car and lower the window.

The nearest cop steps in, his eyes hidden by a pair of jet-black sunglasses. He points at me and asks, "You're from number 65?"

"Yeah?" I reply.

He looks around, like he's keeping an eye out for someone, then looks back at me. "Sorry mate, you can't leave. No one in the street goes."

My heart thumps as the world closes in. "What? No way ..."

"We're making a few calls. You need to stay indoors."

"But ... but you can't–"

He leans in. I tense, feeling his dark glasses bore into the back of my skull. "Sorry?" he asks.

I swallow hard, knowing I'm screwed whatever I do. "Get out of my way or arrest me, but I'm outta here. Got that?"

His lip twitches, then his hand lowers, patting his gun gently. "Mate, if you try to leave, there'll be ... consequences."

Paranoia closes in. Is he one of the freaks from last night? He can't be, can he? Or have I finally lost it? My mind races. Maybe he's searching for these nutcases. Or is he cashing in on things by helping them out, making him a prime example of a real cop-out.

Whoever he is, I can't fight him. I can't tell him anything either. That'll make *me* look insane. Getting out of here's not an option. I'll either be shot or locked in a mental ward. I've no choice but to do what he says. For now.

"Got it," I say bitterly.

He pats the window, nods and steps back. "Good boy."

My heart sinks as I put the car into reverse, turn around and head back the way I came.

Another roadblock's at the other end of the street. Luckily, there's a load of cops and sniffer dogs patrolling the Flats, making a clean sweep of the place. The sheer scale of the operation means they're legit. No one, no matter how psychotic, can replicate this.

I bring the car to the side of the road, then fall back into my seat, sighing with relief. Despite hardcore cop back there, I know I'll be safe now. God knows what's going down, but they're on top of it. I sit, exhausted, never more grateful in my life. Finally, *finally*, I know this isn't about me.

I blink tiredly, take a deep breath, then slowly accelerate, heading for Belle's house and feeling a whole lot lighter.

Belle's front door's not locked when I get there.

"Belle?" I call, pushing the door in. "Hey, you there?"

No response.

I step inside. The table's up again and things are tidier, but not much else has changed. I check upstairs, then come back down. No sign of her anywhere. Weird, but nothing about this place surprises me now.

I lock the door, throw the keys onto the couch and drop down next to them, exhausted. I yawn loudly and flop to one side, ready to forget everything and do what I've always done.

Follow my dreams.

I open my eyes sleepily.

Golden sunbeams still shine into the room. I yawn, then stop, confused. They're streaming in through the opposite window. I frown curiously, then look at the clock on the wall.

Five o'clock.

PM.

A lump forms in my throat. I sit up, rise and head to the window. The park's empty. Only hardcore cop's left, having moved in sight of Belle's house. He's way down the street, but still standing by his car, and still on the lookout.

I should feel safe.

No way. Not with him around.

A loud ring erupts.

I jump and whirl back.

Belle's smartphone's on the table. She must have brought it down this morning. At least it's working and I can call for help, but my chances of being believed? Zilch.

I quickly answer it. "Hello?"

"Hi," a young woman says back. *"Is Belle there?"*

"Yeah listen—" I begin.

"This is Kirby from HR," she cuts in. *"Can you tell her to ring me back ASAP?"*

"Yeah okay—"

"Let her know that her last payslip was on the 28th," she presses. *"She didn't have any leave left to cash in. Her termination's final."*

"Okay but—" I begin, then stop. A framed photo of Belle and me sits by the TV. Reason hits and I frown. "Hang on, what? She lost her job?"

"Three months ago," comes the reply. *"Happens when you don't turn up to work for weeks. She keeps saying we owe her money. We've called a few times. She hasn't answered."*

"Three months?" I say, confused. "But I've seen her heading off in the morning for work."

"Not to us. If you can let her know, that'd be great. Thanks. Bye."

"No, wait—"

Click!

The phone goes dead.

I lower it slowly, thinking this over.

Three months? That was before Belle bought this place. She'd been talking about making big bucks for big dreams. What's she playing at?

I look out the window and into the backyard. A rotting tree stump stands in the middle of it.

Fragments of my dream return.

"That," Mister Nero *says, "is what you must beware of."*

My mind whirrs as a theory builds. I bite my lip, sickened. God, I hope I'm wrong. Being right'll crush me to the bone.

There's no choice.

Grimly, I head outside.

The backyard's a dump. Belle said she's been too busy to work on it 'cause of her job. Now I know that's garbage, just like this place.

I walk up to the tree stump, then turn and look back at the house. The paint's peeling on the back door. Several scratch marks are by the handle. A ladder lies nearby, tipped sideways.

Yes, that makes sense.

I pick the ladder up, placing it against the wall. Sure enough, the ladder lines up perfectly with the scratch marks.

"So," I whisper, looking over the ladder's dirty steps, "you used this to get in, didn't you?"

Footprints are in the soil nearby. Handprints too.

The grimy hand that had slammed the backdoor shut last night had been dirty. That same dirt's still on my shirt.

"It's you," I whisper, picking up a thick wooden plank and opening the back door. "The whole time."

I step into the laundry, feeling much stronger. Slowly, I move in, using the plank to push the toilet door open.

Nothing.

Quietly I turn, place my free hand upon the laundry cupboard's handle, then yank it open.

Tap!

A mop falls out, hitting the floor loudly.

I reach for the cupboard's other door and try the handle.

Locked.

Annoyed, I raise the plank and strike the door fiercely. Once, twice, three times, I strike harder and harder. Finally, the handle breaks, the door swings open and a large shape falls out, slumping to the ground.

A body.

His dead bloodied face stares up at me, frozen in terror. Our eyes meet and I inhale sharply, knowing who he is. The cop who'd been standing behind his hardcore buddy when I'd tried to ditch this dump.

I recall the old lady from the Flats. *"It's this place, y'know. It sends people crazy."*

Hours later she was dancing in the street.

An eerie voice crackles behind me. *"Hiiiiii-deeeesssss…"*

Slam!

I whirl around, facing the door. A shape cowers before it.

Just who I expected.

I draw a sharp breath, clutch the plank tightly and murmur, "Hello Belle."

Last night's horrors return.

"Get-out-of-my-face!"

She'd had no time to wash the dirt off her hands before pushing me out of her room. The grime had rubbed off on my shirt.

She scampers to the side, cowering in the shadows as she covers her face, hiding from the sunlight. Small and pathetic, she gurgles sickly. "Can't be found, can't be found …"

I glance at the body on the floor. "He went looking, didn't he?"

She gurgles again. "No choice. None on the periphery."

"Periphery?" I echo, thinking hard. What the hell does she mean? Sanity?

More gurgles.

Creeeeakkk!

The front door slowly opens. Soft footsteps move in. A shadow looms from around the corner.

I brace for the worst.

A growl follows as the old lady in the nightie appears. She sneers cruelly, no longer a blissed-out street-dancer.

Now she's holding a hunting knife.

Bang!

The back door's kicked open and a man steps in. He's also from the midnight street party, minus his whizzing drills, but looking crazy enough to screw things up on his own. He grins hungrily. "Oh, dear, dear, dear. Not 'savouring' him for yourself, are you Bertha?"

I step back, raising the plank.

The old woman, Bertha, ignores him, looks at Belle, and speaks croakily. "Good choice, Dronus. You've hooked in a bloody good catch." Her eyes catch mine. "You're quite a fighter, luvvy." She smirks. "What's wrong, dear? You know we're not the problem." Her voice lowers. "You are."

My mind tingles. There's truth in her words. Too much so.

She cackles. "You've always been an outcast. Never fitting in. Wallowing in pain but forever denying it. The world hurts too much. That's why you're a writer. You're hiding from your ..." She glances at a mirror, sneering " ... demons."

I follow her gaze and tremble. The mirror's cracked, no doubt from Belle trashing the house the other night. A jagged streak ripples through my reflection, cutting it in half. My temples throb as my headache grows. I struggle to fight it, battling on two fronts.

Within and without.

"You've always run from life," she presses. "Never thinking you were good enough. That's why you ended up at the Flats. The place where everyone goes, eventually. Into the ground."

I shudder.

"Flat friends versus *flat* friends," she spits. "Those who didn't want to play hit the ground running."

She steps in, bringing her face right up to mine. Her hot breath hits me as she stares deep into my eyes, gazing into my psyche. Her gaze flickers. I know her. No. More than that. We're linked. She and I are one.

"Yes," she hisses. "You've never seen yourself as normal. Only defective. That, my boy, is where we come in. You see ... you summoned *us!*"

"Wha ...?" I whisper.

Reality shifts, the world wavers and my stomach churns sickly.

She looms over me, snarling hungrily.

Leaving me ready to drop.

The man gives a mocking laugh. "Welcome home, son."

No …!

A wind gust billows in, wafting through the lounge. The breeze rises and falls, then a soft ruffle below averts my gaze. There, I see on the floor, my reason for living. My saviour in my darkest hours, in the dead of night, when all else has fallen into the shadows. My greatest love in defying the pain and horror of everyday living, helping me rise above it. My supreme desire and my legacy forever.

My stories.

The pages turn in the wind.

"The story goes on," I whisper.

I glimpse outside. The grey clouds are parting, revealing patches of blue sky beyond.

Light in the darkness.

My strength returns as I look back at the old woman, staring into the face of death. "You're not in my mind, lady." I point the plank at her. "I'm in yours." My tone strengthens. "I'm who *you're* afraid of turning into. *That's* why you're hiding in the shadows. You're scared of yourself."

The man gives a hollow snicker. "Cheat. You're breaking the rules boy." He points at the dead cop. "Just like him. He gave us a headache, so we gave him one back by ramming the point home. Right between the eyes."

I step back, defiantly. "Where's the rest of your Flat friends? Too scared to join the party?" I pause. "Oh yeah, the cops' outside. Can't risk a street fight, can you?"

He sneers at the woman. "He's a strong one, Bertha."

"Dangerous," she murmurs in thought. "He's far too risky, Bernie." She shakes her head. "No, there's only one way he can make the cut." She raises the knife. "Now hold still love, this won't hurt, if you don't struggle …"

The man steps in, blocking her path. "No! I want the honours!"

"Back off Bernie, he's mine!"

"It's always you! My turn now!"

"Like hell!" She goes to move around him.

He cuts her off.

She swipes. He arches back, dodging the blade. She lunges with the knife and he grabs her wrist. Belle scurries aside as they struggle savagely. The blade rises high, then low, then between them. He whirls her around, smacking her into me. I hit the wall and fall sideways, dropping the plank as she lunges back at him. She grabs his wrist once more as they glare, hiss and spit at each other, before ...

Squelch!

I cringe, seeing the hilt of the blade up close and personal, sticking out from his stomach. He staggers back, clutching the knife, groaning, "I hate it when she does that ..."

He's booted through the toilet door, slumps heavily over the bowl and lies still.

She steps in, reaches over the body and grabs the knife's handle, wrenching it out, then wipes the bloodied blade on her dress, smearing it red.

"Clear that up," she orders Belle. "If it's one thing I hate, it's a bloody mess!"

Belle nods cowardly.

Bertha comes for me. "Now hold still luvvie ..."

The knife moves in.

My heart pounds, instinct takes over and I grab the plank, leap up and belt her in the face. She wails and falls back, spitting blood. I strike her in the stomach, then the chest, before ramming her into the wall. A trickle of blood flows from her lips as she slides down it.

"My word, you are a *bad* boy!"

I snarl, ready to kill her. My grip tightens on the plank as I raise it, ready to bat-her up.

Rooooooooooooowwwwwww!

I look through the open blinds and out the window. A car sweeps by, heading for the Flats. Two more follow.

Police cars.

Their flashing sirens hit me like a smack to the brain. I blink, shake my head and recoil, watching their glow flicker past the blind's pull cord in the ultimate 'Silver' lining. I'm not like Bertha. Not now. Not ever.

Shakily, I drop the plank, retreat through the kitchen, turn, run into the lounge and bolt for the front door, set on reaching the cops.

Scampering sweeps behind me.

Belle.

She leaps on my back, we crash to the floor, she rolls me over and clamps her slimy, dirty hands on my throat. Choking, I reach for the coffee table, grabbing my laptop.

Smack!

She arches up from my blow, then roars and lashes out, belting me viciously before hurling the laptop into the wall, smashing it. Savagely, she grips my neck once more. I gurgle loudly as my vision swirls and shadows fall, leaving only her glaring eyes of demonic fury.

Bertha staggers over, draped in blood, clutching her stomach with one hand and her knife with the other. "Good girl, Dronus. That's a very good girl ..."

She looms in.

"Belle!" I wince, choking.

Belle pushes harder.

"Belle ...!"

I gaze desperately into her eyes, knowing that the real Belle would never do this. No way. She's my friend. My best friend. We've been through so much. She's fighter. She always has been. No, I believe in her. I believe ...

Believe ...

Believe ...

I peer deep into her fury, pushing through her darkness, terror and hate until ...

There!

I see it. A flicker. A spark. A glimmer of hope pulsing in her raging depths. Hidden, but indestructible.

Belle.

The *real* Belle.

Her gaze flickers as our sparks link. For a second, just a second, we see each other for who we truly are. Not animals. Not killers. Not psychos, but people. Real, thriving human beings who'd never let anything bury us, no matter how bad. I see it all. Her cheekiness. Guts. Defiance. The hell-rebel fighter. She's still there, submerged in the shadows.

She gasps sharply as her spark rises.

Bertha's blade sweeps in.

Belle's spark plummets as she cries out, whirls around and smacks Bertha back. The old hag recoils as Belle reverts to Dronus and lunges. Howling in rage, she grabs the knife from Bertha's grasp, swipes hard and–

Slash!

Thump!

Bertha's head hits the ground and rolls over, landing upright inches from my face with a startled, horrified gaze.

Belle drops the knife and backs off, swamped by her inner demons.

I push myself up, cough a few times, then splutter, "Trust you to take a stab in the dark."

Bang!

The front door's booted open.

Belle's head darts up as hardcore cop steps in, gun raised. Savagery takes over as she grabs the hunting knife, charging in.

Bang!

The bullet whizzes past my head, scraping it, then hits Belle straight through the shoulder. She wails, arches back, hits her head on the table and slumps heavily to the floor.

"Belle …" I whisper, slumping down with her.

My heart pounds as she and I lie staring at each other, ignoring Bertha's grotesque head standing nearby, gazing sickly between us. Belle's gaze links with mine. Slowly, her lips curl into a small grin, then our hands rise as one, interlocking fingers in a bond we've always shared, and always will. That's so Belle, I figure. She's always told the world to get stuffed. She can't be crushed, no matter what.

Our eyelids start closing, ready to pass out.

Thump!

We open our eyes briefly. Bertha's head's slumped sideways.

Belle gives a little smile, as if to say, 'That's what happens when you get a head off yourself.'

"Yeah," I whisper. "Moving out's a real bitch."

And then, like Bertha, our heads drop into dead silence.

***

"Storm's fading," Mister Nero says as we stand under a silver cherry blossom.

We're holding pink cups of red liquid. The guests nearby talk happily, all dressed in bright colours.

"Salmon tea's nice," I say. *"At least we can enjoy it now."*

"Yes." He takes a sip. *"Strong, isn't it? Just like you, my boy. Well done. Well done, indeed."*

I smile back …

… and wake up in a hospital bed.

The light pierces my eyes. I blink, blocking it out, then open them again, wincing. I groan, groggy, confused, and riddled with pain. My vision swirls. It's bright in here. Much too bright, but anywhere's better than Belle's house.

A pretty nurse stands over me.

"Welcome back to the world," she says.

"Thanks," I reply huskily.

"The doctor'll be here in a minute. There's water by the bed. Drink slowly."

"Sure."

She smacks the end of the bed with her folder, grins and walks out the door.

I struggle to sit up, then sip the water. It's refreshing and cool. I put it down and lie back glumly, thinking about what's happened. About Belle, Bertha, the Flats, the whole thing's feral. Totally ...

The door opens and a doctor enters the room, smiling. "How are we going?"

I groan wearily. "Nowhere, but hey, that's my life."

He shuts the door, then looks at my charts. "How's your pain?"

"Sick to my stomach," I answer.

"Your medication helping?"

"I guess." I struggle to sit up again.

"Easy ..." he warns.

"Forget it," I retort. "My friend Belle. Where is she?"

He pauses, wary of the answer. "Now's not the time ..."

"Talk or I'll cut your clock off. You know who she is. She took a shot to the shoulder. What's the story?"

He raises his hand. "I get it." He pauses. "She's okay, but ..."

"But what?"

He inhales sharply. "She's got one hell of an inner demon."

"We all have," I reply. "What's up with hers?"

He relents. "She's no longer in hospital. The police are out looking for her."

"Are you serious?"

"Deadly. She couldn't get out alone. Not in her condition. Seems she had help." He nods at the door. "The cops are at the end of the hall, talking to security. They'll be in shortly."

"Do you want to fill me in first?"

"I shouldn't."

"And I shouldn't be here. Go on. Lessen the blow."

He bites his lip. "You got a point." He takes a deep breath and begins. "You knew how bad Scalpehill was before you went in, am I right?"

"Pfffft, doesn't everyone?"

"Yes, but not everything. Sure, there's the Flats where suicides were going through the roof ..."

"Suicides or murders?"

"Both. Undercover cops were sent in but they also fell flat on their faces. All that got reported was that a large group of insane residents, called Scalpers, lived there. Psychotics so good at hiding their sickness that they could be maniacs one second and perfectly normal the next, then switch back again. No one could tell who was a Scalper and who wasn't. Worse was that they knew they were being watched."

I nod, finally understanding. "Meaning the cops needed an insider who was expendable."

"They didn't quite put it that way, and lots of terms were twisted, but yeah, that was it."

"Bastards. So they got Belle and me."

"No, Belle had already moved in. The cops tried watching her but only got hints of what she'd become. They didn't find much, only that she visited your old neighbour, Mrs. Turner, *a lot*. They're guessing she set things up to tip her over the edge, thereby prompting you to get out of there. She did good, you went in, and the police put you under surveillance. They guessed you had a problem with reality, being a writer."

"Pfffft, yeah. So Belle was already sucked in when I got there."

"Yes," he confirms. "They watched you closely and soon found they'd made the right choice, and it paid off."

I hide my smile, not wanting to give him the satisfaction. "So how'd Scalpehill get so bad?"

"We're trying to piece what we can," he replies. "What seems to have happened is that this all started from a single psychotic who's beyond crazy. We've no idea who they are, only that any boundaries they may have once had were obliterated. We call them Patient Zero."

"Hey, they like to scalp people, why not call them the Head Honcho?"

He smiles. "That's a good one." He pauses. "Whatever their name, we're guessing they have an alluring charisma, which is why so many residents fell, either into insanity or off the Flats."

"Sounds like they had the grounding for it. Thank god I got out in time."

"You're strong, there's no doubt about that. We're impressed."

"My mind's still blown."

"You can thank the Scalpers for that."

"So you got them all?"

His head lowers.

"Crap," I whisper.

He speaks hesitantly. "There's a big job ahead. Yes, the Flats have been raided and the Scalpers rounded up. They'll go to a psychiatric facility ..."

"You mean jail?" I cut in.

" ... isolated from each other and assessed," he continues, "but this isn't over. Your friend Belle's still out there, along with several Scalpers and ..." he pauses " ... The Head Honcho."

"Making me a target," I conclude.

"Yes," he confirms. "You'll need police protection from now on. You're not fit medically either, meaning you need rest, starting now."

I sigh wearily. "Fine, you got a point." I yawn. "Any chance of dinner?"

"Lunch, actually."

"I never know what time it is anymore."

"Forget it." He taps his chart in his hand. "You did well. Many lives have been saved. They have a lot to thank you for."

"A house'd be nice," I reply. "Far, far away."

"I'll see what I can do." He smiles kindly and leaves the room, shutting the door behind him.

I lie back, staring at the roof, exhausted. I don't know what to think, or how to make sense of it all. All I've ever wanted was to write a few books and get a house. A little peace for god's sake. Pure and simple–

"Hiiiiii-deeeeeeees ..."

My thoughts freeze and I look around the room. Nothing.

"Hiiiiii-deeeeeees ..."

Slowly and carefully, I inch up.

"Hiiiiii-deeeeeees ..."

The voice is familiar.

Belle's.

Her eerie pitch scrapes against my mind, making me cringe. This could be the drugs in my system. Trauma. Delayed reactions. Residue from the Flats.

Or maybe it really is her.

Under the bed.

My heart thumps wildly.

Cautiously, I turn sideways, raising my legs over the side of the bed and hating every second, but there's no choice. I have to know.

Bracing for the worst, I close my eyes, take a sharp breath, then leap off the bed. The world blurs as I whirl around, smack into the wall's cold, hard surface and slide down it, wailing in agony. A sharp pain goes up my spine as I hit the floor. I fight back furiously, struggling to keep it together until finally, the pain subsides. Slowly, I open my eyes and see under the bed.

Nothing.

As expected.

I tense, fighting against my back's searing throbs, then exhale sharply, look at the room door and wait.

Still nothing.

No one's running in to see what's wrong. I frown. My yell was loud enough to wake the dead.

Poor choice of words.

Memories tingle in my brain.

"Storm's coming ..."

"You summoned us ..."

"We call them Patient Zero ..."

"Welcome home, son ..."

Taunting cackles rise. I rub my temples, searching my mind for something, anything, to counter their hisses. I push harder, struggling through the raging storm, searching, searching, searching until ...

There!

A spark.

Small, lonesome, and flickering with a wavering tendril, reaching out. Filled with hope, I sweep through my inner storm, fighting against my raging undercurrents until finally, I touch it.

Flash!

Several more sparks blow out from it, morphing into golden spheres, each holding a glimmering memory.

Firstly, Mister Nero.

"Well done, my boy. Well done, indeed."

The doctor's next.

"They made the right choice, and it paid off."

Finally, Belle.

"The whole world sucks but we've always bailed each other out. We're a team."

My spirit rises. The doctor has faith in me. The cops must too. Belle always did. Mister Nero as well. Their faith matters. More than anything. They've *shown* me what's real. I'm not dreaming this room up from a mental asylum. Forget about being in Belle's flat, cowering in the lounge in the middle of the night, I'm not there either. This isn't a ghostly dream, minus Mister Nero. I haven't been killed by hardcore cop and floated to god knows where. What's here and now is real. I know exactly who I am.

Sam Silver.

Writer.

The Flats might have swamped Belle, Bertha, Bernie, and god knows who else, but I'm not them. The only way to fight the Flats is to think sharp.

Belle's snarl returns. *"Hi-deeeees!"*

I scoff, undaunted. "Is that all you've got? Come on you bi-"

I close my eyes, forming a glowing mental shield. Steadily, my shadows are pushed back as my sparks grow, illuminating the landscape of my mind.

The voice shrieks, then softens. *"Hi-deeeees … "*

"Get stuffed."

"Hi-deeeees?"

I let loose, belting out with a mental head-butt. The voice howls, then fades, morphing into whispers.

"Hi-deeeees … ?"

"Hi-deeeees … ?"

"Hi-deeeees … "

Bit by bit it fades, until finally, it's no more.

Silence follows.

I sit back against the wall, panting but triumphant. I'll never let this inner crap get a-head-off me. Not now, not ever. I haven't won, there's a long way to go, but whatever happens, I'm ready.

Belle's out there with her Scalpers, and the Head Honcho, whoever that is. They're watching. Waiting. Ready to split my mind in two.

I smirk. Bring it on, I'm up for it. I've got this far on my own, I'm not losing now. I can fight this, I know I can. I've saved myself, I can save others, and I know who's first.

My best friend in the world.

I'm not leaving her behind, I don't care how long it takes. That leaves only one path.

Straight into the howls of Belle.

Chapter Seven

The Evolution of Sam

Static crackles from the speaker above.

"End of the line," the voice says.

The storm outside's grown. The rain lashes against the window, harder than ever as the wind hollers, as if in pain.

I drop the story by the others, knowing there's truth in every tale. All seem real. I feel their resonance linger in my head like a dark melody.

My memory's no closer to returning. I still have no idea who I am, why I'm here or what I meant to do. Meridian's blown my mind for six-six-six. The only cold, hard fact is the body on the floor.

The locked door opposite creaks eerily.

"The truth shall set you free," Meridian states. *"Think aloud."*

"You're in my head, you tell me," I retort. "Go on, what am I thinking?"

Thud!

The window jolts heavily, making me jump. I look up, just in time to see an owl flying off into the storm.

"Don't make me wait 'til dawn. I'm not a morning person."

A tree branch scratches over the window.

Insight hits. "So you're a person? Not a Rambler, Debt Collector or a hell demon? Ooooh, give it away, why don't you?"

The voice hisses. *"Tread carefully ..."*

"Go to hell," I shoot back. "I'm pulling the strings here–"

"You're also touching a nerve."

The static rises.

I ignore it. "Well, well, well, a human. That leaves us with two stories. The first at the funeral and the last in loserville, but things are never black and white, are they?"

"Explain."

I push myself up, standing as my nausea falls. I blink as the room solidifies and my strength returns, drawing the line with Meridian. Logic takes over as I stare up at the speaker, my mind sharpens and I speak bluntly.

"Why make me read through so many stories? What are you trying to tell me that you can't do face to face? Why the torture? What have I done to you?"

Hisses grow over the speaker.

My eyes fall to the painting of the woman on the wall. I look closely. Sure, she's from the nineteenth century, sitting on a rock, with a long white leg protruding from under her skirt. Her hair's short and her stomach's slightly bulging. I stare at her confused as my mind whirls, thinking hard.

Funeral.

Debt Collector.

Rambler.

Galakir.

Ex-Terminated.

Belle.

Belle ...

Belle ...

Belle ...

Flash!

A streak of lightning illuminates the portrait.

I gasp as my insight sparks with it.

"I see the picture," I whisper. "The *big* picture. None of these stories are about me, are they? They're all about *you!* You're *suffering.* This, all of this, is just one big cry for help."

Sharp breaths grow from the speaker.

I glance at the scattered stories on the floor. "Look at who's in them all. Not just Sam Silver, but ..." I stare at the portrait " ... girls! They're all girls!" My voice rises. "Karmady, Belle, Amber, Taron. God even the Rambler was female. So was the Ex-Terminated, what was her name? Ebony Roller. She even said that karma's a bitch."

The breaths sharpen, growing louder.

I press on. "What stands out is that none of those girls were evil. Most were deluded, or sucked in by an outside force, but not evil, and I bet you're not either." My heart thumps, believing in myself now more than ever. "You can take my memories but not who I am. Who I really am." Lightning flashes again. "There's always a spark somewhere. Even in you."

A static snarl erupts.

"Don't be a baby …" I begin, then stop dead.

The last word echoes in my brain.

Baby, baby, baby …'

Everything clicks into place.

"You're pregnant," I whisper.

Scccraaaaaapppeee …!

A sliding metal blade pierces the static.

I'm too engrossed to care. "My god, I totally see it! The truth's not in one story but in *all* of them. Taron at the funeral was pregnant from the monster I once was. Crystal Spinner was a dead child. Karmady was a debt collector who wanted me to pay up. The Ex-Terminated was a bitter, psycho demon who thought I'd screwed her over."

The scraping grows louder.

I ignore it. "You hate yourself and don't want this kid. I'm guessing you were attacked in the bush, hence the Rambler and Galakir stories. You started off like Mojo and Amber but your sanity shot to hell and you ended up in the darkness. You just wanted to curl up and hide where you couldn't be found, just like psycho-Belle." My voice rises as I step in. "So, who's the father? I'm getting the blame but I know it's not me." I glance at the body. "Is it them? Are you framing me for the killing? Sure, you could set things up and drive me nuts, that'd set things up real sweet but …" I pause. "Why choose me? The only way you could do that was if …"

Lightning shoots by again, illuminating the tree outside.

A tree overlooking a house.

Now I get it.

" …You've always been close," I finish.

Silence.

"You *were* in the stories," I realise. "Karmady Wheeler. Crystal Spinner. Ebony Roller. The names fit. I know who you are! With names like Wheeler, Spinner and Roller, you can only be–"

"Saaaaaaammmmm …!"

A shadow looms over me.

I whirl around.

The corpse is standing by the window, breathing heavily, with half its face peeling off.

A mask.

A long lock of hair falls out from under it, belonging to a woman. A bloodied hand reaches down, pulling the jagged knife from her rib cage. The blood's real but hasn't come from her. Her body's lined with thick padding, meaning …

I swallow hard.

She's killed already.

Maybe there's a body in another room. Maybe–

She moves in slowly.

I inch back.

Her foot hits a device on the floor, lighting it up.

A phone

"*Sam-Sam-Sam …*" the overhead voice whirrs from the speaker.

The screen's littered with digital buttons, all with dozens, if not hundreds, of pre-recorded sayings, no doubt linked to the speaker and ready to go. Another app's below them, where anything typed in can be spoken digitally. No doubt the phone's been on a low light setting up until now, covered by the body and out of sight.

The blade glistens in the moonlight, flickering between light and dark. Her grip tenses, growing tighter as her seething grows louder, then …

The knife blurs as she lunges, holding it high.

I lunge back, grabbing her wrist. The blade scrapes my cheek, stinging it. We fall on the desk, knocking the lamp sideways and sending the fan thumping to the floor where the front casing splits off, rolling away. I push her knife hand back fiercely, grimacing as a lightning streak highlights her wide-eyed raging fury through her peeling mask. The knife comes closer, I push back hard, then cry out as we roll from the desk, fall heavily onto the carpet and roll apart.

She leaps in, seizing my throat with one bloodied hand and raising her knife with the other. I choke hard, my eyes bulging as I struggle furiously. My arm stretches sideways, grasping for something, anything, to belt her with. Gasping in agony, my fingers stretch to the phone, hit the screen, touch a button and then-

Flash!

The lights in the room activate.

Meridian blinks, startled, and her grip weakens.

Whirr!

The fallen fan hums to life.

I struggle sideways and grab it.

The knife swoops in.

I'm faster. "You're fan club says hi!"

Bang!

I smack it against her head. The metal blades rip into her face, splattering me in blood. She screams and smacks it away as I scramble out from under her, retreating over the bloodied carpet before rising shakily to my feet. Snarling, she blinks the blood out of her eyes and follows.

I step back, my hand slides over the desk and …

There!

I grab the granite Sam Silver plaque, pulling it in. Defying its weight, I lash out with it, blocking her knife before belting her in the stomach, then the head. She recoils, screaming, then lunges, swiping again. I duck the blade, my grip slips and the plaque thuds to the floor. I jump back as she swoops in, trips over it, slides on my stories and hits the ground. The knife flies forward, sweeping in for the open fan.

"Crap-"

I leap on the wooden desk. The knife stabs down, hits the middle of the fan, cuts a live wire and then-

"Raaaaaaaaa-!"

She shrieks, jolting wildly from the sizzling shockwaves. Her whole body jerks up and down like a burning puppet on a string, shaking violently as the scorching heat sweeps through her, melting her inside and out, boiling hotter and fiercer until …

A loud click follows as the safety switch kicks in and the fan dies with the lights. Darkness falls as she comes to a smoking halt, twitches, then lies still.

It's over.

I swallow hard from the safety of the wooden desk, then look around, knowing the room's short-circuited. I should be able to leave.

Slowly, I put my foot onto the bloodied carpet and step down.

Nothing.

Carefully, I inch around Meridian and make for the door. Step by step, I head for it, creeping through the shadows until finally reaching it. Slowly, I grip the handle and then …

"Noooooo …!"

I whirl back, just in time to see Meridian reaching out, touching the phone.

My heart thumps wildly.

She hits a button.

"Oh cr-"

Bang!

The door explodes with a roaring blast, blowing me back across the room in a furious rush.

Booby-trapped.

The world blurs, then returns with a vengeance as I smack into the wall, almost splattering against it, then slide to the floor and hit the ground wailing, sick to every broken bone in my body. I gasp in agony, feeling every searing inch of rippling razor-pain. Somehow, through the haze, anguish, agony and nausea, I see Meridian fall back down and slump to the floor, twitching.

Finally, she's still.

I blink sickly, fighting my body's raging torment. Wincing, I lower my gaze to stare ahead. Through the darkness and horror, glistening in the moonlight, I see the one thing that's always given my life meaning, more than anything else.

My plaque.

Sam Silver. Writer.

My eyes move up from the plaque to Meridian, lying motionless in a pile of papers.

Stories. About me.

She got her wish, I realise. She wanted to be a part of them. Now she finally is.

Shadows stretch in, drawing me into oblivion. I should be scared. Terrified, but no, just the opposite. My heart glows with a lone spark, knowing that I'm no longer in Meridian's story.

She's in mine.

My spark glows as the world falls away.

Leaving only peace.

***

"Can you hear me? Mate, can you hear …?"

The voice rises as reality returns. Slowly, I open my eyes. Two hands are examining my neck and face. I can just make out their uniform through a hazy blur.

A paramedic.

I blink, taking this in, then look around and cringe. I'm still in the blood-stained study. Two more paramedics are behind him, and the cops are here too, both uniform and plainclothes.

I start to sit up. The paramedic raises his hand. "Easy. You've had a rough night. You're quite a fighter, y'know that?"

I try recalling what's happened. Sick memories of Meridian and her stories surface. Anything before that's still a mystery, but inklings are rising.

The paramedic looks up at another man. "Two minutes, Trident."

He moves sideways.

The man, plainclothes, kneels before me. "You're looking pretty good for someone who's had the shock of their life."

His badge shows he's a cop. I look to a stretcher in the corner. A body's on it, covered by a sheet. Meridian's mask lies on the floor nearby.

"Is she-?" I croak.

He shakes his head.

I push myself up, ignoring the pain.

He raises his hand. "Hold it."

"Get stuffed."

I push his hand away, roll over, get up on all fours and scramble to the body, wincing in pain.

"Hey-!" he snaps.

He reaches out.

I'm faster, wrenching the bloodied sheet away.

A hideous corpse stares up in a mask of sheer terror.

Meridian.

Not a voice, black spirit or wavering entity. A human woman. Solid. Real. A person with a name. A name I know. The clues had been there in the stories. Karmady Wheeler. Crystal Spinner. Ebony Roller.

147

Now she lies before me.

Turner.

Mrs. Turner.

My neighbour.

The paramedic clasps my shoulder, guiding me back to the stretcher. Flinching, I go with him, watching as she's lifted and carried away. I glance briefly at the papers on the floor, then ask Trident. "What's the story?"

"Not the end of yours," he answers. "We'll get you checked over. You'll be fine." He nods at the severed fan. "God knows there's been enough shocks for one night." He helps me back on the stretcher, then looks up at the paramedics. "Let's go."

They move in, picking my stretcher up. I flinch at the jolt, then wince as I'm carried out the door.

The rest of the night's painfully long. I'm taken to hospital and examined so many times it feels like a hundred, all while fading in and out of sleep. I'm told it'll be a while before the drugs are out of my system. They take ages to wear off, and there are huge side effects, but at least I'm right about one thing. I am Sam Silver. I'm a writer, not a killer. The stories I'd read, however, were all written by Mrs. Turner,

I'm taken to a private room. There's no window, which sucks, but I'm told I won't be here long.

Trident arrives soon after. He fills me in, to a point. The cops have only scratched the tip of the iceberg on what's happened. They've learnt that Mrs. Turner's husband went missing a few days ago. She'd been hiding her psychosis for years and had finally snapped, killing and hiding him in the cellar. She'd then targeted me, baiting me to her house. Forensics found a white powder on an empty glass in her living room. Upon analysis, they found it to be a memory suppressant. She'd then knocked me out, dropped me in her study, splattered it with her dead husband's blood and then posed as the corpse on the floor. She'd also gone to my house, stolen my name plaque and then put it on the desk over me to mess with my mind.

The cops were impressed by how she'd used her phone to control the house's tech. She'd learnt a lot from her husband, who'd been a cutting-edge electrician, and she'd sure shown him a cutting edge in the end.

The scale of her setup's incredible, but baffling. Why target me? What have I done? Trident's as baffled as I am but assures me he'll get to the bottom of it. He tells me to rest and says he'll be back soon, before leaving the room and closing the door behind him.

I rub my eyes and yawn, too frustrated to sleep. Wearily, I grab the morning paper from the dresser, then wince as a ripple of pain shoots down my arm, thanks to my stupid injury. The paper's also a little wet, like a hot coffee cup's been placed on it, leaving heavy stains that have soaked through the pages, wiping out bits of articles. Too tired to care, I ease back and read.

The front page says interest rates are set to rise. Below it's an article about school funding. The second page is about the Hollywood red carpet. I glance at the article beneath it, then stop dead.

'Missing girl found in dumpster.'

There's a shot of that dumpster in an alleyway. Another shot's beside it, showing a pretty, young woman with short brown hair. I frown. Her face is familiar. Hauntingly. I know her but can't think how. Worse still, parts of the article are stained, cutting bits out. I read what's left.

'...was found by a Council worker at 5:30am. Ms ... (Name stained out) *'... went missing three nights ago and has been taken to Carrington Hospital for serious injuries. Investigations are underway to see if it relates to her sister ...'* (Name also stained out) *'... who was on a local bus that disappeared two weeks previously, before the vehicle was found in the hills with no sign of its passengers ...'*

I sit up quickly. My body throbs wildly, but I don't care. I look at the paper's date, then ease up. It's from two days ago. That makes sense. Mrs. Turner must have read it and thought up a story. Simple.

I sigh, satisfied, and keep reading, delving deep into the article.

Barely noticing a cold breeze waft by.

I read on.

The breeze grows. A sick stench rises. I look up, grimacing. The odour's foul and must be seeping in through the air vents. Weird. A plumber's probably playing around with a pipe and stuffed up.

A wet, sticky blob hits my nose. I flinch and sit up. The blob's cold, and sure not water. Another blob follows, then another and another.

I wipe it off my face and look at my hand.

It's red.

Blood red.

I look up at the ceiling and gasp at the ...

"Bloody hell …!" I whisper.

The roof's filled with blood.

Slimy, wet, dripping blood.

I quickly move to get out of bed, then freeze.

Waves of slippery, red ooze are trailing down the wall. They rapidly reach the floor, stretching out for me.

Like long tendrils.

My heart pounds as I slide backwards onto the bed, touching the paper. My mind races, recalling the article and then Meridian's story. How much did she make up about that missing busload of people? Either she'd been lying or telling the …

Another drop hits my cheek.

I stagger out of bed, stumble to the door and turn the handle.

Locked.

What the hell? Trident hadn't locked it.

I bang hard. "Hey, get in here! Anyone! Now!"

No response.

I keep banging. "Come on, get in here! Move!"

Nothing.

I thump harder. "Hey! Hey …!"

Still nothing. I kick the door angrily. This is a damn hospital for god's sake. Why aren't alarms going off? What's …?

I stop and think. Maybe there's a lab upstairs. There's been a system glitch and a blood bank's overflowing. Must be a pretty big bank if there's this much blood. Could be down to medical research. Everyone's run off to help. Yes, that has to be it.

I limp over to the bed and hit the emergency buzzer.

The lights fizzle and die.

No power.

Same with the phone.

Makes sense. If the power's out there's nothing to stop a blood bank upstairs going into the red.

The stench grows.

I whirl around.

All four walls are flowing with blood. I look at the first. Slimy long trails are twisting, turning and parting. Slowly, they form letters.

Making a single word.

'Sooooon.'
Part of a Meridian story returns.

He stares straight at me, peering into my eyes.
With recognition.
He grins grotesquely, then speaks in a deathly low monotone.
"Sooooon ..."

I freeze, rooted to the spot.
"No way ..." I shudder.
Most of the letters drip away. What's left forms another word.
My lips part, reading it. It's not 'soon' but ...
"Son," I whisper.
I recall Meridian's stories and what I'd said to her afterwards.
"You're pregnant."
All her stories were related to jilted women or mothers and children. She was shielding me from my ...
"Father," I say softly.
The wall's bloodied word flickers back. *'Son.'*
I swallow hard. This, all of this, is down to who I truly am.
His son.
Meridian's child.
Their offspring.
I steady myself against the bed, quivering. I'd caught a glimpse of Mrs. Turner's body right before the paramedics had taken her away. She'd looked old, but had the strength of a woman decades younger, just like the old lady in the Galakir story.
Oriana Shepard.
'I'm fifty-two years old.'
The story had said she'd looked as old as the pyramids.
My thoughts break as a stream of blood flows onto the floor, touching my hand. I flinch at its icy tingle and try breaking away. The ooze holds me fast, refusing to let go.
"Wha-?"
A jolt shoots up my arm, straight into my head, igniting memories and blowing my mind. Memories that aren't mine, but those of others, revealing everything.

151

I watch, transfixed.

Mrs. Turner, a *young* Mrs. Turner, had been walking through the bush. She'd stumbled, fallen and tumbled into a dark ditch.

The dead rim of the Pull-Pit.

Thereby summoning the Galakir.

He'd surged in, swamping her, feeding on her hysteria and growing stronger, but not by much. She was too tough for that. So he'd used her in another way. To venture into our realm, he needed an extension of himself. Since she was no good, he'd used her to create a vessel.

A son.

A child within her, to manipulate from the very beginning.

She'd fought back against his ferocious spirit, struggling fiercely. Her defiance paid off until finally, his shadowy, black mist retreated, leaving them both exhausted. There, she was left to lie among the twisted, rotting branches, with a jagged mark upon her stomach. True, she was now with a child, but one with free will.

Yet it came at a high price.

To resist the beast, and to protect her child in the only way that a mother could, she'd sacrificed her mind, leaving her broken beyond repair, never to be whole again.

Nine months later, she was strapped to a stretcher just after giving birth. She'd screamed at the staff for her child but went ignored as she was wheeled to the psychiatric unit. Filled with tears, she was placed howling into a strait-jacket, plagued by demons she'd never be free of.

Not long after, that child was adopted by a sweet young couple who gave him all the love in the world.

A child, granted the name, of Sam Silver.

My new mother beamed when meeting me, kissing my forehead lovingly while I'd smiled back, reaching for her face. Her love had been real. A love that the Galakir could, and would, never know. Thanks to her, I was shielded from his eternal rage.

Meanwhile, he'd watched, and waited, from the hills overlooking the city, preying on who he could find and scrounging off their lifeforce. Such sparse feeding was enough to keep him in this realm, but too weak to sire further offspring.

After a time, he grew strong enough to journey to the city's outskirts, but only at night, seeking his son. He never ventured too far in, knowing that hunters could easily end up as prey. So he'd lurked in the shadows for many moons, retreating into his rotting Pull-Pit at each sunrise, stewing in his hate until night returned.

He never found Mrs. Turner or me. Both of us stayed hidden for decades. She'd been locked up tight while I was free to become a writer, not knowing my true nature. She, however, yearned for all that she lived for.

A mother's deep love for her child.

Alongside that, she'd held another dark desire. Possessed by sheer, raging, vengeful hate, she swore a black oath to ensure my father's annihilation. Such was her revulsion for him and her love for me that her psyche split in two, and she would forever float in the hazy grey realm between light and dark. She loved and loathed me, just like herself. She was both the Mojo trying to help me, and the scornful, psychotic Ex-Terminated who wanted healing and revenge at the same time.

Leaving her, as a Meridian.

Sheer deceit allowed her to pass her hospital medical tests, allowing her release. Over the ensuing years she found a husband and a home. Finally, from afar, she tracked me down. She'd stayed close, moving in next door. Watching. Waiting. Split between love and hate.

When lifted by light, she swore to protect me from him. To give me a fighting chance to lead a normal life. When her howling rage swamped her, she vowed to see me dead, just to get back at him. Another part of her wanted us working as a team to wipeout my father together. Whatever she wished, she couldn't approach me directly, not without alerting him too.

For years she hovered next door. Finally, her psychosis grew too strong, attracting him to our suburb.

Forcing her to act.

A few nights ago she'd seen the weather reports showing a storm coming, meaning he was closer than ever. She couldn't leave me alone if he were nearby, nor could she tell me the truth, knowing that would tip me over the edge, giving him the advantage. So she took me captive, unsure whether to kill me, protect me or use me as an ally. Breaking the truth gently was her only way to ensure success, so she wrote several stories and wiped my mind to do so.

Only parts of the Galakir story were true. There was no ghost-girl Crystal, that was totally made up. As for Amber, yes she'd had a sister who'd vanished on a bus in the hills, that much was true. Amber had then gone searching for her but got well and truly dumped on by life's garbage in the end.

Mrs Turner had set up her house nicely. When her husband found out what she was doing she killed him, then finished her traps. She achieved in seizing me but failed in winning me over. That's not surprising, since she had no real plan of how to use me in the end. Ultimately, events backfired, killing her.

The ooze grows colder against my skin.

Enough's enough.

I smack my hand against the wall, then slide it up and down the cold surface. A little ooze rubs off. I rub it a few more times, then smear what's left on the floor. Strangely, the smears rise by themselves, turn around and waver back in for me, forcing me to recoil.

Last night I had a choice to pick which story was true.

Now there's none.

A groan rises from the corridor.

A long dragging sound follows, like one leg's being pulled behind the other.

Shakily, I reach up to the bedside dresser and grab a draw handle to pull myself up. The whole thing wavers and the draw flies out, hitting the ground and spewing objects everywhere.

Along with a pair of scissors.

God knows what they're doing in a hospital room drawer. Maybe they're used for cutting bandages, but who cares? They'll do as a weapon.

Kill or be killed.

The dragging draws closer.

My fingers wrap around the cold metal as I rise, step up to the wall, turn my back and lean against the concrete. The icy surface tingles through my shirt as I grasp the scissors tightly. Slowly, I raise them to head height.

Soft, sharp breaths come from behind the door.

Click!

The door unlocks.

Creeeeeeaaaaak!

The handle slowly turns and the door's pushed in,

I watch, quivering, as a long shadow looms into the room, touching the blood-stained walls.

Now or never.

I whirl around and lunge, the scissors held high.

The figure steps in and simply smiles.

I lash down savagely. The blades hit their target, squelching in deep. I wince sickly as my vision grows hazy, the world swirls and then …

Flash!

My mind blows into oblivion.

I'm no longer Sam Silver. No longer human. No longer a writer, or reader, of stories. No longer shifting between my mother and father in a psychic tug-of-war. My mother's won, saving me from my father in the only way she knew how. By turning me into what he could never be. The fine line, the wavering boundary, between deep humanity and pure, unrelenting rage.

I am a Meridian.

About the Author

Sam Silver is a steadily rising author who's having a blast as his career takes off. He holds three university degrees, all writing-related, and has been involved in various literary festivals, stalls, writing groups, and has conducted speech-writing workshops.

He's done everything from rock-climbing to axe-throwing, archery, and competition dancing, and has experienced the best life has to offer, which usually comes from the local Sushi store down the road.

Legend Has It is his fourth novel after Burning Embers, Meltdown, and Incipience.

He lives in Perth, Western Australia.